# YOUNG CARDINAUD

# Young Cardinaud

GEORGES SIMENON

*Translated from the French by*
RICHARD BRAIN

**A FOUR SQUARE BOOK**

Originally published in France as *Le Fils Cardinaud* in 1942
First published in Great Britain by Hamish Hamilton Ltd. in 1956

\*

FIRST FOUR SQUARE EDITION 1959
Reprinted September 1966

*Four Square Books are published by The New English Library Limited,
from Barnard's Inn, Holborn, London, E.C.1
Made and printed in Great Britain by
Hunt, Barnard & Co. Ltd., Aylesbury, Bucks.*

# CHAPTER ONE

HE was being carried along, like a cork on the tide. His back straight and his head held high, he gazed in front of him and everything he could see mingled intimately with all that he heard and all that he felt, with memories, with thoughts, with intentions.

He was pleased, pleased with being himself, with being there, with what he had done since his first communion which had taken place in this same church, pleased with what he had done since his marriage—it was on the Saturday that seven marriages had been celebrated at Notre-Dame de Bon Port alone . . .

There was no need to bend his head or lower his eyes, his son was at his side, a little fellow of three years old in a sailor suit, gazing in front of him as solemnly as his father.

And it was a solemn joy that Cardinaud felt; the sound of the organ was solemn too, and the smell of the incense, and the silence of the thousand people packed into the church for the Sunday High Mass.

In unison they all made the sign of the cross, knelt down, stood up again, or else, with heads slightly inclined, knocked on their breasts, and there were some, like Cardinaud, who opened their mouths . . . One could not distinguish their voices . . . They were fused into the wave of sound which the bourdon of the organ sustained:

'*Agnus Dei, qui tollis peccata mundi . . .*'

Twenty or thirty children, up aloft, in rows, staring fixedly at their missals, were singing in high trebles:

'*Agnus Dei, qui tollis peccata mundi . . .*'

5

Cardinaud had been one of them too, in the same church. He was dressed in black, as he was every Sunday, as were all the men he knew, the members of the parish who occupied the important pews. Behind, the crowd was crammed together, those who only come to Les Sables-d'Olonne in the summer and for whom Mass is a diversion, women in their holiday clothes, with painted nails, some with bare feet in sandals, young men in shirt-sleeves . . .

He could see all of this, without turning round, he could see it all, could live it all, the comings and goings of the dean and the two curates before the altar, the little hurried footsteps of the altar-boys in red and white, the clink of the cruets. For he had served at Mass too.

The time, the place, the actions, everything linked together, everything combined to make up the clear, comforting whole of a fine Sunday, the first Sunday after Whitsun, Trinity Sunday.

'*In principio erat verbum . . .*'

His lips were moving in time with those of the celebrant and there was no need for the Latin words to bear any precise meaning.

'*Unigeniti a Patre, plenum gratiae et veritatis . . .*

' *. . . Deo gratias . . .*'

Before long, from the pulpit, the dean, with blue-veined cheek and slightly quavering voice, had begun his sermon with a text from the Epistle of St. Paul to the Romans:

'*O the depth of the wisdom and of the knowledge of God! How unsearchable are His judgments and His ways past finding out! . . .*'

A grating of hinges. The beadle was opening the great door. The air changed in quality, the light grew harder and the footsteps on the paving-stones of the church sounded like the tide, the organ played at full blast, the bells rang out and at that moment a tiny hand slipped itself into Cardinaud's hand, that of his son who was lost to view in the half-darkness of legs and skirts.

6

'Good morning, Monsieur Mandine . . .'

'Good morning, Madame Béliard . . .'

The syllables weren't actually spoken, because they were in church, and then in the porch, but you could see people mentally pronouncing them as they nodded to each other with a touch of Sunday solemnity about them.

Everyone looked happy. The girls were wearing white dresses and ribbons, and smelt of eau de cologne. The boys had been to have their hair cut. Groups were forming on the square in front of the church, outside the furniture shop. The *Charcuterie Parisienne* was closed. An Italian with a little yellow barrow was selling ices.

'Good morning, Monsieur Cardinaud . . .'

He was being greeted not only by the local people who had known him as a child or a growing boy, but by notabilities such as Bodet the lawyer, or the deputy mayor, or the owner of the ice-house for whom an open car was standing waiting at the corner of the Rue des Halles.

The child stumbled.

'Watch your step, Jean . . .'

'Where are we going?'

'To buy a cake . . .'

As on every Sunday morning. Slowly, solemn. First of all, they did the traditional walk round by the Remblai. The sea was a virginal Maytime blue, waiters were bustling about the terraces and as one passed one breathed the smells of beer or apéritifs.

'Good morning Cardinaud . . .'

One day . . . At any rate, in a few years' time . . . Why shouldn't he do so, he too, build a villa beside the pine-trees, like Monsieur Mandine and so many others? Why should the sea be exclusively reserved for the summer visitors?

He was still walking, as if in a procession, and he stopped automatically at a certain terrace. It was here that there

7

was the best band, and the owner shook him by the hand as he went by.

'How are you? . . . And this little fellow? . . . Julien! Look after Monsieur Cardinaud . . .'

Julien knew what he had to fetch, a vermouth for Cardinaud, a small glass of redcurrant syrup for the kid.

'Thank you, Monsieur Cardinaud . . .'

Some boats, very far out. A swarm of bathers in the dazzling whiteness of the breaking waves. A waltz. A persistent violin.

He drew his watch from his pocket, a gold watch, and he could tell in advance that, to within a few seconds, it was half-past eleven.

'Come on, Jean . . .'

The child bumps into passers-by. They turn left, mount a few steps. A sugary smell. The three Mademoiselles Dufour, in white, their hair as golden as puff-pastry, are busy behind the counter.

'The same as usual, Monsieur Cardinaud?'

As usual, too, there is a *madeleine* for Jean.

'You going to carry it, little man?'

He says yes. They slip his first finger under the red string, but a little further on his father takes the box from him because the child is holding it lop-sided and the cream might . . .

'Don't drag your feet.'

The streets grow less lively. They reach the Place de la Liberté, huge and shadeless, where little waves of overheated air alternate with fresher breezes.

There it is, a hundred yards away, Avenue de la Gare. He could go there with his eyes closed. Mechanically, he lets go his son's hand and, while still walking, he takes his key from his pocket. His neck is pink and shiny, because his collar is too stiff. He will be able to take off his jacket, hang it on the bamboo coat-stand, on the right of the passage.

In a way, all that he has already spent of his Sunday is with him still, the organ, the incense, the dean's voice and the more profane waltz on the Remblai, the airy rustling sound of the sea on the sand . . .

It's a modern house, of red brick. The door is of varnished oak, real oak—he had insisted on that—with a brass handle and two panes palely tinted yellow behind a design in wrought iron. A modest brass plate: 'Hubert Cardinaud' . . . He didn't add 'Insurance', because his office is not here, but on the quayside. Not to mention that he is not yet quite acting in his own right. Not that he is just an employee of Monsieur Mandine's either, since there is talk of making him a partner in the firm . . . Some people already say:

'Monsieur Mandine's partner . . .'

He smiles. He bends down ever so slightly, an old habit which goes back to his childhood, to look through the keyhole: the door at the end, which leads into the yard, is open, so that the passage is very light, with its yellow and red tiling, the pitch-pine door on the right, which goes into the sitting-room, then the dining-room door. He knows the smell of the roast joint will welcome him, and the crackling of the fried potatoes in the bubbling oil; he knows . . .

'In you go . . .'

The child climbs the two steps.

'What are you waiting for?'

A sudden impatience in his voice. He wouldn't be able to say why. Or rather . . .

'Marthe!' he calls.

It's not the smell of the joint but of the joint burnt, and a blue mist emerges from the kitchen. What's more, a draught can be felt blowing, upstairs, in the bedrooms. Why should the bedroom doors be open?

'Marthe! . . . Go on, Jean! . . .'

9

He still doesn't want to hurry. And he even hums a tune. He hangs his straw hat on the hall-stand. He catches a glimpse of himself in the glass and is satisfied with his reflection.

'Where's Mummy?'

The kitchen is a room glassed-in on one side, which extends the house by encroaching on the yard. It's more clean, more practical. It was his own idea . . .

'Marthe! . . .'

The dining-room is empty. The table isn't laid. The baby isn't in its cradle. What could it be, on a Sunday? . . .

In the kitchen, the smell of burning is stronger, the smoke thick, and Cardinaud opens the oven, burns his fingers as he pulls out the dripping-pan on which there is nothing left but a sort of black coal.

'Where is Mummy?'

'Do be quiet, please . . .'

He thinks better of it. His voice grows gentler.

'Mummy'll be coming . . .'

'Where is she?'

How can he tell? It's a terrible feeling, the same as when, God knows why, he thought he had tuberculosis and went to see a specialist. Just as he entered the waiting-room, it seized him, in the chest, all over, a wave, a sudden emptiness, a softening, a panic.

'Stay here, Jean . . .'

He climbs the stairs three at a time. The two bedroom doors are open, the window at the back too, the curtain puffed out like a balloon.

The beds have been made. He opens the wardrobe with the mirror. On the top shelf there's no sign of Marthe's latest hat, the one she had made for Whitsun.

'Marthe! . . .'

There they both are, she and he, in a gilt frame which stands out on the wall-paper of little flowers, and Marthe, just as the photographer suggested, because that's how it

10

ought to be in a wedding photograph, is leaning her head slightly towards her husband.

It can't be true . . . What could . . .?

Where would she have gone, on a Sunday morning? And with the eight-months-old baby! Could something have happened to her father? Let's see . . . She's done the beds, the bathroom . . . She's put her joint in the oven . . .

So it's less than an hour ago . . . Someone rang . . . Someone told her that . . . She dashed upstairs . . . Otherwise she wouldn't have left all the doors open, as she loathes draughts. She's always calling out:

'The door! . . . Can't you feel the draught? . . .'

She picked up the baby, Denise, or 'Pinkie' as they call it . . . But she didn't take the folding pram because it's still in the hall . . . If she'd gone far, she would have taken the pram, as she isn't strong and the child is heavy . . .

He is back downstairs again. Jean looks lost and keeps saying:

'Where has Mummy gone?'

He tries to smile and he makes a face like someone about to burst into tears. Then suddenly . . .

Someone has just knocked on the door. They're rattling the letter-box . . . Here she is, thank God, she must have, for some reason or other . . . All the same, she might have left a note . . .

Now that it's all over and he hurries to open the door, he is trembling even more from the fright he was in, and all at once his whole body grows limp.

He opens the door. He has already begun to say . . .

'You're home again, Monsieur Cardinaud . . .'

'It's you, Mademoiselle Julienne? . . . My wife's left a message for me with you, has she?'

Mademoiselle Julienne, who lives next door, the Herbemonts' daughter: well-to-do people who keep a magnificent Pyrenean dog.

You can't tell her age. She isn't old, but she's no longer

a young woman, and her face has the grave beauty of a nun's face. She is very gentle. People are always saying what a gentle and good person she is . . .

'Do come in, please . . .'

Into the drawing-room, of course. The Herbemonts are the sort of people who . . .

'I mustn't stop, because of the baby . . . Your little girl, she's . . .'

'Is the baby in your house?'

'Just over half an hour ago, Madame Cardinaud rang our door-bell. She asked me if I'd keep the child until you got back . . .'

'What did she tell you?'

'Nothing . . .'

'But surely . . . Do come in, mademoiselle . . .'

They can't stay there, on the doorstep, in the bright sunshine, and people are already looking at them, from the bar opposite, for example.

'She must have had some bad news, I don't actually know . . .'

'She didn't say anything to me . . .'

'Did she look upset? . . . Please do come in . . .'

The drawing-room smells of wax polish and linoleum.

'Excuse me asking you all these questions, but I'm . . .'

He doesn't know what he is. He mops his brow. He no longer feels steady, no longer feels his own self; it seems to him that everything is wavering, everything shifting, fading away.

'I was going to ask you another . . . I'm sorry, it's time for your dinner . . .'

'It doesn't matter, Monsieur Cardinaud . . . If he was to take Jean too . . .'

'I want to go with Mademoiselle Julienne! . . .' the child decides; sometimes he goes to tea with the people next door.

'I'm so sorry . . . Just while I run round to my mother and father-in-law's . . .'

'Not at all . . . I'm only too glad . . .'

He forgets his hat, retraces his steps. The door slams rudely shut because of the draught.

Why, yes, why not have left a note on the table? Just like Marthe! If it had been him . . .

He's walking fast, too fast, slackens his pace because people are turning round to look at him and he is ashamed of it. He should have taken his bicycle. It's silly to go on foot in such bright sunshine when . . .

And it is a long way, right down there, to the Avenue de Talmont, two houses past the cemetery. The little trees only give tiny patches of shade. An old woman is returning from the cemetery, with her hands folded in front of her.

*Justin Vauquier, Stone Mason . . .*

Blocks of stone in a yard, sacks of cement, bricks, ladders and carts with their handles up in the air, everything covered with a fine white dust, like the house which is modern and jerry-built.

He rings the bell. No one answers. He pushes open the door. At the Vauquiers' the whole place is always in such a mess that no one thinks of closing the door and anybody can walk in . . .

'Anyone in? . . .'

It doesn't seem like a house where some disaster has just occurred. A cat comes out of the kitchen and rubs against Cardinaud's legs. A fire is burning, but nothing cooking on the stove.

'Anyone in?' he repeats.

A voice calls, from upstairs:

'What is it?'

'It's me, Mama . . . I'm coming up . . .'

He goes up. How can people live in such a mess? A house which cost a lot, but has nothing to show for it.

13

There are even some doors which haven't had their second coat of paint! A bedroom with the bed unmade. A woman as dark as a Spaniard, painted like some of the holiday-makers, already wrinkled, with her hair dressed like a wig.

'Come in . . . What's the matter?'

'Isn't Marthe here?'

'No . . . Why?'

What was his mother-in-law doing when he arrived? She must have been on her bed, which still bears the mark of her body and has a novel with a brightly coloured cover lying on it.

'I don't know . . . I thought . . .'

'Isn't she at your house?'

Silly fool! As if he would have bothered, when Marthe was at home, to . . .

'Where's Papa?'

He has always found it difficult to call that loutish work-man, always stinking of alcohol, 'Papa'.

'I wish you could tell me, son . . . Soaking himself some-where or other, as usual . . .'

She's probably bought some ham, or some cold meat, and she's going to eat it by herself at one end of the table, without laying the cloth. Nothing, no one, in that house, is ever in its right place.

Madame Vauquier—her name is Estelle, which is ridicu-lous for a woman of her age—doesn't care.

'You look hot . . .' she states bluntly.

'I'll go and look at home . . . Maybe . . .'

'At home', in the language of the household, means 'at Cardinaud's parents' home'.

But there isn't a chance of it! If anything had happened to his father, they would have come and told him of it at church, or on the café terrace, or at the Dufours' cake-shop, since they know exactly what he does on Sunday mornings. Besides, he called at his home at half-past nine,

14

before High Mass. His mother was putting some cherry tarts in the oven. She said to him:

'I'll keep you a bit . . .'

She keeps him a share of everything she makes. She claims that Marthe doesn't know how to cook. As if it mattered! The question now is . . .

'You off?'

Yes, he's off! He plunges into the dusty sunshine, onto the endless avenue where he is the sole passer-by, where there is only a dog, near a gaslamp, rolling with its paws in the air.

Let's see . . . If Marthe merely told Mademoiselle Julienne . . .

It's no use. He's giving himself a headache to no avail. He's passing quite near to his own house. Supposing he went to see? . . . No! He'll go to his parents' first. He is back amongst the cool and shady little streets, past the front of Notre Dame, the closed shutters on the shops.

He turns right, then left, and you can see families at their meals through open windows, you can hear their voices, almost share in their lives.

Here it is . . . Rue de la Pie . . . The shop is shut . . . The house is, so to speak, in two parts . . . They live in the left-hand one . . . He stoops . . . The kitchen, which is the living-room, is at a lower level than the pavement . . . It's like a cellar . . . You go down ten stone steps and the stairs are as steep as a ladder . . .

It's cool. The shade is soothing. The copper pans gleam. The tiled floor is of bright red, the furniture polished, and the tick-tock of the tall grandfather clock can be heard . . .

'What, you?' exclaims the elder Cardinaud who has his back turned and is eating stew with peas and carrots.

There is no tablecloth, but a brown oilcloth which Cardinaud has always known. His mother has still got her coarse blue linen apron on, the same blue that the sailors in Les Sables wear.

15

There are only the two of them, with Nestor the cat, sitting in Father's wicker arm-chair. The five boys are married. Two of the three daughters as well. The third is a nun in a convent at Fontenay.

He makes one more attempt at a smile.

'Marthe isn't here?'

His mother looks at him. His father goes on eating. Is there any need for an answer? What would Marthe come here for? Has she ever set foot in here except when she has to, on certain birthdays and at New Year? She's not the sort to come and pay calls at Rue de la Pie!

For two pins, Mother would sound plainly pleased to ask:

'Has your wife gone?'

But no! She says it seriously, lowering her head, because there are some things one doesn't joke about.

'I can't make head or tail of it . . .' Cardinaud tries to explain.

He is embarrassed. They could have answered him:

'It's what you wanted, isn't it? . . . We've told you so often enough . . .'

They could have gone on to say:

'Well, well! So you come to us with your tales of woe? . . . You were perfectly happy going off on your own to become a gentleman and we're lucky if we see you for a few minutes, with your son, on Sundays before High Mass . . .'

Though none of his brothers has become a basket-maker, like Father, they have remained local people, working-men: Lucien is a joiner, Léon does a little business making caps, Arthur . . .

The stew smells good, and has an indefinable smell with the smell of the street underlying it.

'What's she done about the children?'

How is it possible? He hasn't said anything. He hasn't yet envisaged anything exactly and yet here they are, talking quietly to him about his wife's departure as if it were . . .

'But, Mother . . .'

'You tell us she's gone. And I'm asking whether . . .'

'It can't be true! . . . Look, she did the bedrooms, she put the joint in the oven, she . . .'

'Didn't she say anything to anybody?'

Old Cardinaud, who always wears a sailor's cap on his head, even indoors, gets up with a sigh and goes to the pipe-rack to choose a meerschaum with a long cherry-wood stem. He has glanced at his wife. That probably means:

'Leave him alone . . . You can see that . . .'

That what? That the boy is shattered, that he's trying hard not to burst into tears, not to shout, stamp, bite, as he used to when he threw a fit of temper as a kid.

Isn't it ludicrous? Isn't it enough to drive the most reasonable of men wild?

If only there had been something, a row, anything you like? But no! This morning Marthe was gay, at least she was the same as usual, neither gay nor sad, and she had said yes when her husband had suggested going for a walk in the afternoon towards La Rudelière.

She had a new dress last week. She had put it on to go to Mass at eight o'clock and she had taken it off to do the housework. She had brought home the joint, as she did every Sunday. She used to get it at the Market on her way.

A pall of silence, surrounding him, now. His mother was finishing her meal and, unconsciously, she was taking care not to bang her fork against her plate. Father was standing at the foot of the steps, facing the street, his head at the level of the pavement from which waves of heat were wafted in.

What could one say? What indeed? Just that one knew nothing! Cardinaud rises painfully, like a man worn out, and he sighs:

'Oh, well . . .!'

'Where are you going?'

'I'll go home . . . Perhaps . . .'

His mother doesn't believe it.

'Why not have a bite to eat first? There's some stew left and there are some cockles . . .'

'I'm not hungry . . .'

'Come on, eat up . . .'

How does it happen? It's true that he isn't hungry. He's in a hurry to go home to see whether Marthe has returned, in a hurry and afraid at the same time, and yet, perhaps because of this fear, he puts his elbows on the brown oil-cloth, just as when he was a child, he gulps down the cockles which his mother opens for him one by one and places, all pink and mauve, pink like something new-born, on his rough china plate where knives have scratched a thousand tiny lines.

The pendulum swings to and fro in the clock-case. The dial is surrounded with copper figures representing the ages of life.

'Have some butter . . .'

From the red earthenware butter-dish which they put under the trough of the pump to keep it fresh.

'Arthur will be coming, with Juliette and the children . . .

He knows very well. He knows all about that. The others, on Sunday afternoons, reunite, in their shirt-sleeves, in the kitchen or in the yard, and the babies' bottles are warmed up in the *bainmarie*, and the wives exchange recipes for cooking or jam-making.

But he . . .

He turns his head away. His mother has understood and puts a steaming plateful of stew in front of him.

'Eat up, son . . .'

He shakes his head. No! He can do no more. He needs must, simply must burst into tears. He would have wished

18

to avoid that, but he is too miserable, too upset, it's too stupid, too unfair . . .

Father and Mother look at each other. He himself has gone and leant against the wall, his head between his arms, and from time to time they hear the harsh sound of a sob while his shoulders heave and sink.

'Perhaps it's nothing that can't be put right . . .'

Then the words which hurt his throat to speak:

'But she never used to see anyone . . .!'

True enough! It's not because Marthe has a half-crazy mother and a father whom you find staggering down the streets or declaiming in cafés . . .

'She hasn't even got any women friends . . .'

Even as a girl, she used to go along the road, all by herself, with her exercise-books under her arm, and they used to say she was proud.

He wasn't yet fifteen when he fell in love with her, not as one loves a woman, but as one loves an unapproachable creature, as, at the time of his first communion, he had loved the Virgin.

'Come on, son, eat up now . . .'

He was eating. What he ate had the taste of tears and of his childhood. Then he decided, getting up:

'I must go and see . . .'

'What have you done with the children?'

'They're with Mademoiselle Julienne, one of the neighbours, very nice people . . .'

Oh, yes! That was always the way! He hadn't thought of taking the children to his own home, but he entrusted them to the Herbemonts, very nice people, people who . . .

'Off you go, son . . . Be sure to tell us if there's any news . . .'

Father himself has said nothing. He is an old man. His trousers sag at the knees and the seat of them hangs far down on his thighs.

When the boy has left, he sighs and carefully shifts the

19

cat so as to take his place in the creaking wicker arm-chair.

The house in the Avenue de la Gare, seen from a distance, hasn't changed. Nor from closer to. Through the keyhole, it's obvious that nothing has happened inside.

He will have to go and collect the children, since one can't expect the Herbemonts to . . .

How empty it all is! The colours look harder. More like a house that's never been occupied, where the plaster is scarcely dry.

Yet he himself planned every detail, watched it all being carried out . . .

'When we have a house of our own . . .'

They did. They almost did, just as he himself was almost a partner of Monsieur Mandine's. But there were still instalments to pay for six years. The day after to-morrow, actually . . .

He wasn't thinking. He was standing there his arms dangling at his sides. Then he took a few steps. Then he stood motionless again.

He was empty; there was no other word for it. And because he was empty, material anxieties seized hold of him again; he went sadly upstairs into the bedroom, ran his hand along the top of the wardrobe with the mirror. It was there they put the old note-case where they kept the money. It ought to have contained, beside the family papers and the marriage lines, the three thousand francs which he would have pay on the house on the fifteenth of the month.

The note-case was not in its place. Cardinaud climbed on a chair, not caring about the blue velvet with which it was covered, the velvet to match the curtains.

The note-case had only been moved. It was a little further to one side, open. It still contained the marriage lines, but the three thousand francs were missing.

# CHAPTER TWO

THE day refused to end. It was drawing out its life, all the more splendid and majestic now that a copper-red sun had sunk into the sea and a light that threw no shadows spread out from the very world itself.

At nine o'clock, beside a hemless sea, and on the freshly virgin sand, a few people were still bathing and far out on the water could be seen the blood-red cap of a woman swimmer. On the Promenade, the crowd was moving slowly along, a crowd from the poorer districts this time, which came to survey the terraces where people were still eating. And the waiters were raising the striped awnings, the bands were tuning up, and lobster carcasses were sticking fast in the sauce on their dishes.

The slightly disquieting purity of so beautiful an evening penetrated indoors. Cardinaud, seated in the kitchen all by himself, watched the lime-dressed courtyard wall, in front of him, turn slowly from pink to green. What was he eating? He didn't know. He caught himself looking with surprise at the piece of cold veal on the end of his fork, and two or three times he turned round abruptly.

His nerves were on edge. He kept thinking she was there. He thought he could feel her presence, he expected to hear her rather flat voice saying:

'Hubert . . .'

More often than not she would add:

'Keep an eye on the children for a moment, will you?'

Because children can't be left by themselves. That's why they transform one's whole life. Now he was listening. What was she doing, upstairs? When he had come down, she was sitting beside the cradle; the blinds were lowered; the room was all in semi-darkness; Jean was asleep, without any bedclothes over him. She was entirely dressed in black. She had said:

'So long as I'm home by eleven o'clock . . .'

She was a stranger; she wasn't from the district, not even from Les Sables. But she was accustomed to looking after children. Her name was Trichet. Did she have a Christian name? When he had asked her name, she had replied, pouting her lips:

'Mademoiselle Trichet . . .'

He wasn't eating. He wasn't doing anything. He was in a state of suspense like the light outside which the night could not succeed in absorbing. Against the wall of the yard stood a broom. He imagined Marthe's hands, her silhouette, the sound of the broom on the uneven stones of the yard and the next moment he suddenly felt his eyes moist and warm.

Earlier on, he had called at the Herbemonts'. The house had a strange smell, the smell of a rich house. He couldn't have said what it belonged to, to the carpet on the stairs, or the big blue vase which was used as an umbrella stand, or the dark wood of the wainscoting: it was rich, or rather prosperous, and he felt he wanted to walk on tiptoe, to talk in undertones.

'Come in, Monsieur Cardinaud . . .'

Old Monsieur Herbemont, who had a white goatee beard, rose from his arm-chair to shake his hand.

'Not bad news, I hope?'

'No . . . No . . . That's to say, my wife has had to go away for a few days . . . A relation of hers . . .'

And Mademoiselle Julienne, who was showing Jean a photograph album, gave her sympathetic approval:

'I understand . . . Where will you send the children?'

'I shall keep them at home . . .'

Old Madame Herbemont was pottering to and fro in the

next room, the door of which stood ajar. The dog was dreaming. In the white marble fireplace there was a gas-stove of a kind Cardinaud had never seen before.

'I might be able to put you onto someone to help you . . . A very nice woman who looks after children at the youth club . . .'

That's how it had come about. The air was filled with the blare of horns and motors; cars and buses followed each other head to tail, and all the people from the country round, in dark clothes and with red faces, poured into Les Sables. But he was saying 'Thank you', stammering, clumsily picking 'Pinkie' up in his arms, then not knowing how to get his key out of his pocket.

'Would you like me to help you?'

'No, thank you . . .'

He closed all the windows, all the doors, without know-ing why, as if thereby the house would be less empty. He lit the gas to warm up the four o'clock feeding-bottle.

'Now be good, Jean . . .'

And then, just as he was giving the baby its bottle, the bell rang. Like a fool, he started. As if Marthe would ring the bell! She had her own key!

'Good afternoon, Hubert . . . I've come to see if you . . .'

It was Juliette, his brother Arthur's wife. There she stood, hatless, pushing the pram with her two children in it.

'Come on in . . .'

'I can't, because of the pram . . .'

She didn't ask if Marthe had returned, as if it were already agreed that she would never return. He fully realized how it had happened. They were all at his father's. They talked about him and Marthe.

'What'll he do with the children?'

And Juliette had suggested:

'I could easily take them for a few days . . .'

She was saying as much.

'You have only to bring them round to me, Hubert . . .'

23

No! Neither to her, nor to anyone else! He didn't know how he would manage it, but he would keep them. Besides, Marthe would never have trusted her children to Juliette.

*'She lets them play on the ground, with anything they lay their hands on!'* she used to say. *'One day there'll be an accident . . .'*

'Thank you, Juliette, it's very kind of you, but I've already asked someone to come . . .'

'Oh! . . . All right . . .'

She was hurt. It was silly of her. She began pushing her pram again and moved off into the sunshine.

Another void.

'I want to go for a walk, Daddy!'

'In a minute . . .'

Two or three times, he had caught sight of himself in the glass. He wasn't doing it intentionally, but he was staring at himself. He was serious, dignified, calm. He was all right. He was keeping cool. He was bearing everything in mind. Jean's slice of bread and honey, the baby's napkins to be changed; then he could hear footsteps on the pavement and he went to open the door to Mademoiselle Trichet just as she was putting out her hand to ring the bell.

For her it was all quite normal, naturally enough with those who are used to standing in for others. She said:

'By the way, I shan't be able to stay the night here . . . You see what I mean . . . With a single man . . .'

And straight away she began picking out the household articles she required, arranging things.

'Baby has six feeds a day now?'

She opened the larder, found what she needed for getting the dinner. He was following her round, gauche, unable to help. He wanted to explain and she had no need of his explanations, but it gave him something to do.

'For Jean, in the evening, we usually . . .'

He had of course thought of going to the station, and

questioning the man who punches the tickets. How would he have noticed one woman rather than another on a Sunday when thousands of people troop past? It wasn't as if he knew Marthe!

Besides, Cardinaud had the feeling that she hadn't gone away, that she hadn't left the town. He wouldn't have been able to say why. She was somewhere about, and if he knew how to look . . .

He still had half an hour ahead of him. He set off on his bicycle. People were out in the fresh air on the terrace of a small café. Monsieur Herbemont, on his doorstep, was waiting, as he did every evening, till his dog had done its business. He said good evening. He reached the part near the cemetery. But he rang at his parents-in-law's house in vain. Everyone was out. Anyhow, why would Marthe have been there?

The whole thing was pointless, and equally so to return to his parents' house, where they were sitting out on the pavement with some neighbours.

'Where are the children?' his mother asked at once.

'I've got someone to look after them, a woman who's used to . . .'

'Juliette suggested . . .'

'It's very kind of Juliette, but she's got enough to do already with her own . . .'

He went round by the sea front. That served no useful purpose either. Figures were beginning to shade into each other, cars were leaving, hundreds of men and women were sitting out or walking slowly along, girls humming, young men turning round to look at them, some of them wearing flowers in their hats.

He climbed the stairs on tip-toe. Mademoiselle Trichet opened the door and on the landing she simply said:

'I'll come at seven tomorrow. Do they deliver your milk?'

'We leave the milk-can on the doorstep. The dairywoman comes round at half-past six . . . The coffee's . . .'

'I found it . . . Good night, sir . . . I'm taking the key I found on the nail behind the door where the apron is . . .'

Marthe's key. Marthe hadn't taken her key!

And yet he went to sleep. At half-past five he woke up and reached out his arm towards the empty place. He was behaving quite naturally. It seemed to him that his life had already taken on this new rhythm for a long time.

He went downstairs, noiselessly, lit the gas, warmed up the six o'clock bottle. Jean spoke in his sleep, some unintelligible syllables, then in a single movement turned over on his other side.

There was a low chair for giving the baby its feed. The blinds were still lowered. Some trawlers were returning to harbour.

He was holding the warm bottle in one hand, supporting Denise's head with the other as she looked gravely at him.

Every day it would be the same thing . . . He would not hand over the children to anyone . . . It wasn't the first time he had put a baby's napkin on . . .

He shaved and dressed.

'Mummy . . .'

'I'm here, son . . .'

'Where's Mummy?'

'Mummy's gone on a trip . . .'

'What's she gone to get?'

What has she gone to get?

'Lots of things . . .'

'Toys?'

'Toys as well, yes . . .'

He washed and dressed his son and the boy was ready when Mademoiselle Trichet lit the fire in the kitchen.

He was saying good morning, as on other days, walking at his usual pace. Someone—the woman in the corset-shop —had said as he went past—and he had heard her:

26

'Young Cardinaud raises his hat with a fine air . . .'

He passed through the swarming activity round the Fish Market, entered his office at nine o'clock exactly, changed his coat and laid his fountain-pen on his table. Bourgeois, the clerk, came in whistling.

'Good morning! . . .'

He never showed much respect although he was only twenty-two, ten years younger than Cardinaud, and he was lazy.

'Is the boss in?'

He looked at the door of Monsieur Mandine's office and Cardinaud began to tremble.

That was going to hurt most of all. He had already been thinking about it the day before. He didn't cease to think about Marthe, of course, but he was also thinking of this step he would soon have to take . . .

The windows looked onto the quay. The clerks were separated from the public by grilles, as in a post office. Monsieur Mandine and his family lived on the two upper floors and they could be heard going to and fro, then the director's steps on the stairs, the door of the office opening.

Now was the moment. Cardinaud gathered together his papers, waited a few seconds, knocked, and entered without waiting for an answer.

'Good morning, Monsieur Mandine . . .'

He was a little fat man, a *bon vivant*. It was said that he had a mistress at Nantes where he paid frequent visits. Almost all day long he had a toothpick in his hand or between his lips, so that he always appeared to have just left the table.

'What's your news, Cardinaud? How did you enjoy yourself yesterday?'

He asked the same question every Monday, didn't expect an answer.

'Interesting post this morning?'

'Nothing important, Monsieur Mandine . . . On the other hand, I've got to speak to you . . .'

He felt like adding, since he knew what Monsieur Mandine was thinking—his slight frown had not escaped him:

'Oh! it's not what you think . . .'

It wasn't a question of asking for a rise in pay, though two years had already gone by since . . .

'You see, Monsieur Mandine . . . My wife . . .'

It's disconcerting to start a conversation with someone who, as early as nine o'clock in the morning, fiddles with a toothpick.

'My wife has been obliged to go away for a while . . .'

'Nothing serious, I hope?'

'She's had to go and look after a sick relative . . . As a result, I was forced to give her . . .'

He who made it a point of honour not to ask anything of anybody! But hadn't Mandine continually said to him:

'You, Cardinaud, I don't regard as an employee, but as a friend . . . My business is your business, and I won't conceal from you that I intend, one day . . .'

'I've had to give her quite a large sum, several thousand francs. In a couple of days it'll be the fifteenth and I must pay the usual instalment on the house . . .'

'The house?'

It was only to gain time! Monsieur Mandine was already looking out of the window. He was perfectly well aware that Cardinaud had had a house built and had signed agreements to last several years. He had even come to the house-warming party.

'I thought you might be able to lend me three thousand francs; of course, I'll repay them very soon . . .'

A silence. He dared not draw another breath. His employer continued to look out of the window, sighed, rose to his feet, came over to Cardinaud and laid a hand on his shoulder.

'My dear friend . . .'

Cardinaud froze, his throat tightened, he felt that the contact of this hand preluded a new disaster.

'. . . You know the friendship, I may say the affection, I feel for you . . . That's what makes me upset that you have found yourself obliged to make such a request of me . . . I have certain principles to which I hold fast, principles which are the basis . . . Let's see, my friend! . . . It's ten years now that you've been with me, that you've been earning a handsome living . . . Not once have I refused you an increase in salary . . . Yet, here you are with debts . . .'

'Sir, I swear to you . . .'

His ears were red, like a schoolboy's when he is being reprimanded.

'I'm all the more distressed in view of the fact that you have my complete confidence, you can sign cheques on my behalf, you hold the keys of the safe . . .

'Come now, my friend! . . . Think it over . . . I'm willing to forget what you've said to me . . . And if you're temporarily embarrassed, things'll work out all right, within your own family . . .'

Some gentle pats on the shoulder.

'Come now! . . . Don't let's talk any more of these disagreeable matters and hand me the mail.'

The oddest thing was that Cardinaud made no reaction, that he handed over the letters one by one, took notes, discussed the question of the premium for a trawler which had had its engine changed . . .

And he went back into his office and sat down in his chair, near the window, opposite Bourgeois, of whom he only saw the back view and who always had a newspaper or a pamphlet under his blotter.

It was too extraordinary! More extraordinary, almost, than Marthe's leaving! Yes, more extraordinary! Because after all . . . A man like himself . . . A man who had always worked conscientiously, a . . .

Not just an honest man! He was more than that. A

scrupulous man, studiously concerned to do the right thing, to live a good life, to . . .

He was choking and, now and then, stared at the window with a distraught look.

Economies? But he had already made so many—even to cutting down the number of cigarettes he smoked—that the house was already three-quarters paid for!

And here he was, short of three thousand francs, being almost accused, because of that . . .

For after all, why else speak about the right to use his signature and the key of the safe?

He wasn't even a centime in debt! He hadn't ever asked anyone to postpone payment! And now . . .

Suddenly, he took his wallet out of his pocket and his brows grew damp, he felt ill, real pain, in his bones . . .

That was all right . . . Two hundred-franc notes . . . On the first of the month, as usual, he had given Marthe the housekeeping money . . . He never kept more on him than some change and two hundred-franc notes, *just in case*, as he would say . . .

It was the thirteenth . . . Before long Mademoiselle Trichet would be asking him for money for the shopping . . . Actually, she had forgotten to ask for any this morning . . . Perhaps she didn't dare, perhaps she was as sensitive on this point as Cardinaud himself? . . .

In that case? . . .

Footsteps, in the next room. The door of the corridor opening and closing again, a sleek and dapper figure on the quayside, a man's figure, Monsieur Mandine's, as his eyes drank in all the gaiety of a fine morning and a harbour seething with activity, and he moved off slowly for his usual walk.

'Phew . . .' whistled Bourgeois, who got up and went to get a cigarette from his jacket. 'To think there are people basking in the sun on the beach! . . . What's up with you, Cardinaud?'

'Me? . . . Nothing . . .'

'You've gone all white . . .'

There are times when, without knowing why, one is on the point of doing the stupidest things. For a moment, Cardinaud was tempted to ask Bourgeois for some money! Bourgeois, who, by the twenty-fifth, always had to ask for an advance on the next month!

'What were you going to say? . . . You started to say something . . .'

'No . . . Nothing . . .'

'Is something wrong? . . . Is it the boss? . . .'

'No . . .'

He opened the window. Too bad! The boss didn't like it, because he claimed that no work could be done with all the noise of the harbour coming into the office. Some women from the Fish Market were standing, in Sablais skirts, black stockings and country clogs, with arms akimbo, in front of the boats being unloaded, and you could hear them calling out; bursts of laughter rang around.

Till then, Cardinaud had thought . . . It was ridiculous . . . A mere trifle . . . The corset-woman's remark . . . Still, it did mean something . . . It was true that he raised his hat with a fine air, it was because he was conscious of his own worth . . .

He was, indeed, young Cardinaud . . . His father was a humble basket-weaver and his grandfather before him used to weave osiers at L'Ile d'Elle . . . His mother had come for the season, like so many Breton women, to work at the sardine-curing . . .

But he had studied . . . He had won a scholarship . . . He had become . . . Well, it amounted simply to this; he had brothers whom everyone knew in the district round Notre-Dame and in the harbour district, but it was he, and he alone, who was called Young Cardinaud . . .

Raising his hat with a fine air . . . Well, it was rather— it made him blush, made him want to cry—a sort of patronizing gesture for all the common people whom he had left behind but still used to go and revisit, to show them that he wasn't proud . . .

There! And now he was watching a fish-wife taking from under her skirt a fat wallet full of crumpled notes, giving one of them to her daughter, and shouting at her:

'Get half a pound . . .'

Half a pound of what? Not that it mattered. The girl hurried away and, as she ran, her skirt revealed her thighs sheathed in black wool. What did count was that fat wrinkled wallet which Cardinaud had looked at covetously, despite himself, those notes all stuffed in and jumbled up together . . .

A fisherman in blue returned with some litres of wine which he was dispensing to a boat's crew . . .

And he, he, Cardinaud . . .

He laughed nervously and Bourgeois looked at him in surprise. Three thousand francs! He had been refused them! He would have to pay them in! He must give Mademoiselle Trichet some money, not only for the house-keeping, but for her wages as well!

Where was there left for him to turn to? Go and find his father, or one of his brothers? Not just one, but two or three of them, since none had three thousand francs to dispose of all at once, like that . . .

Even his father . . . His savings were in premium bonds . . . He would anxiously await the drawings of the lottery . . . Ask him to sell some bonds?

Cardinaud knew very well what they would think, what they would say behind his back, on Sunday afternoon, when they were all together in the yard or when, like common people, they brought out their chairs onto the pavement to take the fresh air. They would say:

'. . . yet he's too proud to trust his children to Juliette! . . . They wouldn't be well enough taken care of . . . He has to have a special governess . . .

'And he asks us for the money to pay her!'

It was crazy! Only the morning of the day before . . . For it was the day before, just at this time . . . He was standing in his pew, at Notre-Dame de Bon Port. He was singing, listening to his voice mingling with that of the organ . . . He was on his way to the Dufours' and one of the Mesdemoilles Dufour was wrapping up a cake for him . . .

Wait! What happened to the cake? He must have put it down somewhere, but since then he hadn't seen it again. It was a cream cake. In this heat . . .

The day before, he was walking along in the sunshine and there was pride in his step. He was walking towards . . .

Nothing at all! By now he was thoroughly brought low. Lower, indeed, than the fish-wives whom he watched in envy, lower than those fishermen who put their bottles of wine to their mouths like bugles!

He was even envious of Bourgeois, the bachelor taking advantage of the open window to ogle a girl.

'I say! She's wearing one of those pairs of . . .'

He was barefaced, on purpose. He would tell all his adventures at the office, giving full details, particularly the crudest ones, since he knew Cardinaud was as easily shocked by certain words as a girl.

Why did he go on to add:

'What did you do yesterday?'

Just like the boss! Had they arranged it together?

'Nothing . . .'

What had he done? What was he going to do? He was at the bottom of a well!

Three thousand francs . . . Two hundred francs . . . He no longer knew . . . It was no longer a matter of this or that amount, but of his whole life, his personality, himself, Hubert Cardinaud, who had suddenly . . . Crack! Without any warning . . . In full daylight . . . In full sight of everyone . . .

And they were laughing! . . .There were three or four of the fish-wives turned towards Bourgeois who was playing the wolf, while a girl eating some sausage held a piece of it out to him at a distance, calling:

'Come and get it, unless you're scared . . .'

Bourgeois hesitated. He would have been quite capable of going across, if he hadn't been afraid that the boss's wife might be at her window, on the first floor . . . And she was spiteful! Thoroughly thin and spiteful!

It didn't occur to Cardinaud to close the window, to break contact with this world weltering in the vulgarity of its coarse laughter.

They were happy enough! Not long since, that huge woman, Titine, in some corner of the Fish Market, behind a stack of crates, used to . . . With any one who liked, any old ship's captain or any fish-seller! . . .

It was life! It was laughter! It was the sweat of sheer animal pleasure and the sun was made for them, whereas Cardinaud . . .

'Bourgeois, I wish you would . . .'

'O.K.! O.K.! The day you're the boss yourself, I know one person who'll be . . .'

A gesture which meant:

'Who'll be clearing out . . .'

He had no idea, poor fool . . . One would think they were doing it on purpose! Even this car . . . It probably cost a couple of hundred thousand francs! . . . With the hood right down, and red leather seats . . . A young man at the wheel, bareheaded, his shirt-sleeves rolled up, and three women, in summer frocks . . . They were stopping . . . They were looking around them . . .

'Will it make a good picture? . . . Is it worth bothering about? . . .'

'Some sardines, girls?'

34

A point of contact was made. An old woman brought a magnificent live lobster, bright blue in the sunlight, across to the party in the car, and they thought it amusing to buy it; one of the women seized hold of one leg with frightened shrieks . . .

The car started up noisily . . . Further on . . . More photos to take, more fun, more life.

The door suddenly opens, the director's one. How can that be? Which way has he come back? Bourgeois, by the window, hasn't time to adopt a serious attitude.

'So that's it, Bourgeois! . . . Don't mind me . . .'

Monsieur Mandine is wearing light grey flannel trousers, and white buckskin shoes. He's been as far as the Promenade and sat on the terrace of the English Bar to drink a glass of old port, and his breath still smells of it.

Bourgeois bends over his desk. The director is standing in front of Cardinaud.

'Ah, well . . .'

His face looks sorrowful and he's shaking his head.

'You see how it is, Cardinaud! . . . What was I saying to you only this morning? . . .'

There's a whole world of implication in his remark! He goes on shaking his head and heaves a sigh as he sucks his toothpick.

Cardinaud can still hear echoing in his ears the saying one of his schoolmasters used to repeat in that same pitying way:

'Steal a pin and end up in jail . . .'

'You see, Cardinaud? . . . You've got the key of the safe, you're entitled to sign cheques. I've promised you that, one day, you'll be . . . And here you are, in debt! . . . And you come and ask me for three thousand francs . . .'

The director returns to his office. The minute-hand, on the pale black-ringed dial of the clock, no longer seems to move. Twenty past eleven. Suppose it should stay for ever twenty past eleven, that noon should never come . . .

35

Nevertheless, noon comes . . . Cardinaud walks along the shady side of the street. He exchanges greetings. Perhaps, without realizing it, he greets people he doesn't even know . . .

His house, over there . . . Someone's on the doorstep . . . His heart is beating . . . No, now it's stopped beating . . . It can't be true . . . He knows very well that nothing will happen from now on . . .

Mademoiselle Trichet, so dour-looking when she was dressed all in black, has put on a white embroidered apron and a white veil over her head, like a real nurse. She is holding Jean by the hand. It was her idea to bring him out onto the doorstep to welcome his father, and he can now see her clearly urging him gently forward as if to say:

'Go and kiss your daddy . . .'

She has told him what to do, beyond doubt. The child, who isn't used to this, goes forward awkwardly, reaches out both his arms.

'Hello, Daddy . . . I've been a very good boy . . .'

She must have taught him this so that, when his father returned home, he would not . . .

He turns his head away. Does he kiss his son? Or does he not kiss him? His eyes are stinging. He weeps. He hurries past, looking the other way. He pitches like a blind man into the coolness of the passage, because of his tears which confound everything.

Behind him, a strange woman's voice is saying slowly:

'Shut the door gently . . . Gently . . .'

Gently! He weeps gently, facing the yard, his yard, the yard of his own house.

# CHAPTER THREE

HE didn't read the letter straight away, on account of a slightly ridiculous episode, and he almost didn't read it at all. He had heard it falling into the letter-box just as he was preparing to leave the house, at a quarter to nine. He didn't want Mademoiselle Trichet to notice he was in any hurry. He still had a little comedy to perform.

'By the way . . . I was forgetting . . . I must give you some money for the housekeeping . . . Here's a hundred francs anyhow . . . I shall get some change presently . . .'

'I don't need any money, sir . . . I got the things on account . . .'

He looked sharply at her, then glanced away. He had never dared open an account with shopkeepers, for heaps of reasons. First, it's like having debts. Secondly, Marthe used to claim that one never knew how much one was spending by this method, it wasn't like paying out money note by note or coin by coin. Last but not least, to Cardinaud's way of thinking, because of his own childhood recollections, accounts were almost the hallmark of a particular section of society, the privilege of people who are well off.

Quite calmly, without making any question of it, Mademoiselle Trichet had translated the household into the class of people with accounts!

She laid the table for ordinary meals with cloths that they previously kept only for special occasions! She used the dinner service! The whole business was odd, at once pleasant and irritating. She took the initiative in everything. It was her own idea that she should sit at meals with Cardinaud, but, on the other hand, she would wait till he was in his place before she sat down herself.

She had bought some flowers. Probably because, in the families with whom she had lived, there were always flowers on the table. She had even brought down from the bedroom a side-table which wasn't in use. She placed it beside the dining-table, as they do in large restaurants, so that she didn't have to move to serve the food, whereas Marthe used to get up three or four times during the meal.

Awkwardly, he took his leave, murmuring:

'Good-bye for now . . .'

And it was then that the ridiculous incident took place. Cardinaud was walking down the passage and was aware that someone was walking behind him. He didn't like to look round and he was wondering whether . . . He almost forgot the letter, remembered it at the last moment, opened the box, stuffed the envelope in his pocket without looking at it . . .

They were waiting, behind him. He opened the door. Thereupon, like a good boy who has learnt his piece, his son Jean came forward and said, carefully enunciating the syllables:

'Good-bye, Daddy . . .'

And, reaching up on tiptoe, he offered his little face for a kiss.

Cardinaud blushed. Mademoiselle Trichet stood still, watching the scene she had obviously prepared.

'Good-bye, son . . .'

He realized that this was a little ceremony which would be repeated each time he left the house. The governess, with her veil over her head, stood on the threshold with the child while he walked away and Cardinaud wondered whether people had noticed them, from the cakeshop or from the small bar. It was like something from a sentimental film. The little boy watched him walking away and Mademoiselle Trichet waited until he had turned the corner before closing the door again.

People would think it was he who . . . Yet the whole thing, this way of behaving, those flowers on the table, the best tablecloth, the dishes and the soup-tureen from the dinner service, even the white veil over her head, all these discreet attentions were pleasant enough and reminded Cardinaud of life in hospital, after an operation, when everyone behaves so kindly and continues to make things easy for one.

He could already see the sails of a couple of boats at the far end of the street before he remembered the letter. The yellow envelope was one of those trashy envelopes sold in tobacco kiosks; the paper, ruled in squares, had been torn and the words, in violet ink, had been scrawled by someone who wasn't accustomed to writing.

> *'Instead of playing so posh, you'd do better to keep an eye on your wife; she was getting off nicely with Titine's son, at the "Little Green Bar" at midday on Sunday.*
> *'You're a poor cuckold.'*

There were mistakes in it. 'Poor' was spelt with an 'e' and 'cuckold' with a 't'.

He had stopped on the edge of the pavement. He was shocked—in all conscience it was his first feeling—shocked by the vulgarity, by the crudeness, by the mistakes, by the boorish familiarity of it all, shocked by the spitefulness which the note breathed.

He was saying to himself:

'It can't be true . . .'

No, not at the 'Little Green Bar'! He himself, and he was a man, had never once set foot in it. One walked past without pausing. It was on the other side of the seaway, at La Chaume, immediately opposite the ferry. There were three or four little taverns such as you might find anywhere

39

else, with blue-clad fishermen on the terrace, but the last one, painted a lurid green, which gave it its name of the 'Little Green Bar', was more cramped and sordid, with a dubious-looking passage running beside it, and leading to God knows what sort of rooms.

Cardinaud had begun to walk on again, mechanically. He had turned the corner of the quay. As he passed by the Fish Market, he glanced inside, where the auctioneer's voice was ringing out. There was Titine, near some stone-slabbed tables amongst the other women.

He had an urge to go in and ask politely:

'Excuse me, madame . . . Is it true your son's home . . . ?'

They would all look at him and burst out laughing! Titine, who was familiar with everybody, would be equally so with him and fling some coarse joke at him.

He walked on past, entered the office, changed his jacket, placed his pen on the table and went over to close the window which the cleaning-woman had left open to air the room.

He was so preoccupied that he didn't notice that Bourgeois was more lively and hearty than usual.

'Hello, Cardinaud, old boy . . . How's yourself . . .?'

Cardinaud sorted the mail, carefully slit open the envelopes, his thoughts elsewhere. Titine's son . . .

He could picture again a red-headed lad, with a face covered in freckles, who was the only one in the class to wear clogs and always had his pockets full of things to eat. He was said to pinch them off barrows. He never denied it. He used to laugh, with a nervous laugh like a rattle.

It was some time ago, maybe ten years, that he had left Les Sables.

'Psst . . . !'

Bourgeois was calling his attention, indicating the director's door, for Monsieur Mandine had arrived several minutes before and he had not heard him.

With the mail in his hand, Cardinaud knocked, entered, spoke the ritual words:

'Good morning, Monsieur Mandine.'

'Good morning, my dear Cardinaud.'

And he did not even notice the unaccustomed 'my dear'.

'A registered letter from Orleans about the Basset business . . . I'll tell them that unless the doctor's certificate is more explicit . . .'

He wasn't looking at anything in particular. Leaning over the desk, close to Monsieur Mandine's shoulder and his greying hair which smelt of lavender water, he was working through the letters one by one, unconscious of the task, like a machine that keeps on going on its own impulse.

'This is the sardine man with a claim for . . .'

It was finished. He stood upright, collected his papers, moved towards the door.

'Cardinaud . . . !'

He had already reached out for the handle. He only half turned round.

'Come here a minute, old chap . . .'

And Monsieur Mandine rubbed his plump hands together like a man enjoying himself.

'Angry?'

'No, sir . . .'

'Well, then! Don't pull such a long face, old chap . . . Here . . . !'

He took three brand-new thousand-franc notes from his drawer, where they were placed ready, and held them out with a mischievous smile.

'There you are! . . . That'll teach you not to be so cagey with an old friend like me . . .'

For the first time, Cardinaud's eyes were full of mistrust. He should have been saying, 'Thank you', and smiling in

41

return, and there he was, standing rather stiffly near the door.

'Don't look so mournful, for God's sake! . . . You're not the first this has happened to, my dear old chap, and the others haven't got along so badly . . . As for the money, it'll be all right if you pay me back so much a month . . . You can fix the amount yourself . . .'

How did he take the notes? What did he stammer in reply? Somehow or other he found himself back in his office, where he met Bourgeois's amused glance.

He had just realized, suddenly. They knew! People knew about it! People were whispering to each other:

'You've heard about young Cardinaud's piece of bad luck . . .?'

They were laughing! It was so amusing that Monsieur Mandine, who had refused him three thousand francs the day before, when he thought it was only money troubles, was prepared to offer them now that there was a woman at the root of it, and he could make jokes about his assistant!

'Boss in a good mood, eh?' asked Bourgeois.

Cardinaud's face did not relax, carved as hard as stone, and in an expressionless voice he said:

'Will you please get on with your work, *Monsieur* Bourgeois!'

Something had just happened, it would be impossible to say at precisely what moment, but certainly whilst Cardinaud was standing by the door, a sort of click like that of a camera taking a photograph: his features had hardened, had changed in substance, and from now on there was to be no further connection between the interior and the exterior man, between what went on inside and on the surface.

The day before, Cardinaud had wept, several times. Every now and then he had looked at people with anxious, almost beseeching eyes; he had blushed; he had trembled.

Now he was in complete control of his reactions, so calm,

so terribly calm, that it seemed to himself that he had stepped outside his own life.

'Pass me the Mondanel file, will you? Get me 223 on the 'phone. Then you can go and collect the payment due on the Saupiquet policy . . . Get a move on, *Monsieur* Bourgeois!'

He had gone home to dinner, because of Mademoiselle Trichet. He had left her in the bedroom where the blinds were drawn, together with the children, and he was now stepping aboard the ferryman's boat, looking straight ahead, beyond the stone quayside, at the narrow green front of the bar, at its dirty awning, at the three terrace tables bare of customers and the shadowy moving figures inside.

He had known the ferryman a long time, had always known him. The old man knew he had married Vauquier's daughter. He might have asked him whether, on Sunday, not long before midday . . .

The tower of St. Nicholas's Church pointed its sharp steeple into a sky washed pale like a picture post-card, and the white façades of the low houses seemed a fading pink. Some blue groups of fishermen were set here and there in the limpid evening air as if by some stage producer.

The nearer he approached, the more clearly could Cardinaud make out faces, in the half-light of the bar, the darker patches formed by clothes, the white apron of a barmaid with bare legs.

He sat down on the terrace. He did not want to turn round or concern himself with what went on behind him, though musty smells of wine and spirits wafted out to him.

'What's it to be?'

He gave a start. This was already a sort of confirmation of the imputation in the anonymous letter. The girl in front of him was, in fact, none other than one of Titine's daughters. He had often turned round to look at her in the

43

street, in the days when she used to work with her mother at the Fish Market.

She shrugged her shoulders, grumbled:

'When you've quite made up your mind . . .'

'Get me anything, some wine please . . .'

'A *chopine* of Muscadet?'

'Yes . . .'

She must be eighteen or nineteen. Tall and naked under her black dress which was relieved by the white of the apron, she had pointed breasts which shivered at her every movement, a full mouth, red and moist, and impudent eyes.

Cardinaud knew that anyone could have her, just like her mother. From time to time, when he used to see her out of the office window on the quay, he had had thoughts at which he blushed and which made his blood flow more hotly in his veins.

There was whispering, behind him. Someone laughed. A voice said:

'No kidding?'

He didn't know whether they were talking about him and he was embarrassed, ashamed to be there. He was afraid someone from the town might come past.

What would they think young Cardinaud was doing at the 'Little Green Bar'?

'Here you are! . . . One franc fifty . . .'

He pretended to search for some change in his pocket, to give himself time to muster his courage.

'Is it true your brother's back in Les Sables?'

'What's it got to do with you?'

He was staring at the barmaid's feet in their dirty espadrilles.

'I heard that on Sunday . . .'

'My brother's free to come to Les Sables if he likes . . .'

Wasn't it worth going on, now that the first effort had been made, and driving his heroism to the limits? He raised his eyes. No one could tell what it cost him to do so.

'Listen, miss . . .'

Provided only his voice didn't turn to a beseeching whine! . . . And now she had put on a leering smile . . . She had glanced for a second into the half-dark interior, a conspiratorial look which must have meant:

'What did I tell you? . . . Listen to him . . .'

Ah well! Never mind! They were laughing! Hadn't Monsieur Mandine laughed? Hadn't Bourgeois seemed to burst out laughing two or three times during the day?

'. . . I'd like to know whether your brother was paid a visit here, last Sunday . . . A visit from a woman . . .'

Then she did outstep the bounds of decency. Swaying from left to right, with loose hips, one hand in her apron pocket, she jeered:

'Perhaps it was your woman, Monsieur Cardinaud!'

There was a sudden noise, inside, but he could make nothing out clearly.

'. . . Only, if you've come to find them again, you've got here a bit late . . .'

She held out her right hand and repeated:

'That's one franc fifty!'

He rose from his seat and almost knocked the table over. He hadn't moved three yards away before several people, including a fat woman with fleshy features, hurried to the door to watch him leave.

The ferryman was on the far side. Rather than wait for him, Cardinaud walked all round by the wharves and docks.

It was an odd thing, but as he progressed, he felt a sort of gradual calming down, and the words which repeated themselves over and over in his head were:

'It's true!'

That's it! It was true! He knew! He need make no bones about it! Not only was it true, but others had heard the whole story before him, like Monsieur Mandine and Bourgeois!

The whole town, in fact, knew.

'Madame Cardinaud's gone off with Titine's son, Emile . . .'

It was still improbable, astounding, but at all events it was a fact, a certainty.

She had gone away with Emile, Mimile as he was called. Their departure had taken place from the 'Little Green Bar'.

Well, he would find her again.

Just simply that!

His mind was made up.

In his now habitual state of calm, he gave the baby its six o'clock feed. He dressed Jean, who scarcely mentioned his mother any more and said:

'When's Mademoiselle going to come?'

She, too, after all, must know. It was because she knew that she paid him these guarded little attentions!

She would see well enough, by and by, that he wasn't beaten, that he was looking facts in the face.

Once again, that morning, the ceremony of his departure for the office took place, with the girl in the white veil at the door, and Jean watching his father walk away.

'I think, *Monsieur* Bourgeois, I'm going to change the date of my holiday, and, as a result, you'll have to change your arrangements . . .'

He would never have spoken like that the day before. He never liked causing trouble or upsetting people in the slightest. For he knew Bourgeois was intending to leave on the following Saturday for a trip in the Midi with some of his friends.

But he was the elder, the senior of the two, and he was entitled to choose the date of his own holidays.

With the same air of having made his mind up, he went into Monsieur Mandine's room. He had not got the mail in his hand, as he usually had.

'I've come to ask you, sir, if I may start my annual holiday from to-day. There isn't much work at the moment and Bourgeois can manage. I was going to ask you as well...'

A trembling in his fingers, in spite of everything. He had made up his mind that from now on he would see the thing through to the end.

'... I was going to ask if I might take an advance of two thousand francs out of the petty cash ... I shall probably have to meet certain expenses...'

After which, Monsieur Mandine was the more embarrassed of the two! He was the one who couldn't understand, who looked at his employee with a mixture of respect and alarm.

'Just as you like, Cardinaud ... Obviously in the difficult and painful circumstances in which you ... Well, anyway, you understand ... It's my duty ...'

'Thank you very much, Monsieur Mandine ... Bourgeois will bring you the mail...'

The director felt himself obliged to rise and shake him warmly by the hand.

'My dear Cardinaud, you know how fond I am of you ... Indeed, you have my fullest sympathy ... I've been thinking of your children, and your ...'

'Thank you, sir ...'

Three minutes later he was out on the quay, he was a free man, at a quarter-past nine in the morning! Free to go where he pleased! Free for a fortnight, since he had a fortnight's holiday!

Some women in bathing costumes or beach-gowns were on their way down to the shore, dragging their children along, one carrying a striped bag. The heat was beginning to make itself felt. The atmosphere, in the sunshine, was quivering like water on the point of boiling.

He turned down the second narrow street on the left, then into another, which climbed steeply up on to the

47

Remblai. He heard the regular sound of wood being planed, the scrapings of the shavings, and a few yards further on, he entered a carpenter's shop.

'It's you!' exclaimed his brother Lucien.

Lucien was embarrassed. He never expected to see Hubert in his shop at this hour of the day and he wondered what it could be about.

'Sit down . . . Wait a second . . . I'll clear a chair for you . . .'

'Don't bother . . .'

Of all the Cardinauds Lucien was the most plebeian. His wife, Catherine, was the daughter of a sardine-seller who used to push her barrow around the streets, crying the traditional '*La Graude!*' Catherine herself used to sell sweets from a trestle table outside the girls' school. But now they owned a dozen houses in the poorer neighbourhoods, some of them near St. Nicholas's Church.

'Aren't you at the office today? . . . Is it the children . . . ?'

'The children are all right . . . I've come to ask if you can tell me something . . . You know Titine's son . . .'

'Mimile, yes . . .'

Lucien knew, it was obvious from his growing embarrassment.

'Is it true he's back in Les Sables?'

'So I've heard . . . Apparently he was injured and went and hid at La Chaume . . .'

'At the "Little Green Bar" . . .' Hubert put in. 'It was his sister, the barmaid there, who told me . . .'

Lucien looked at him in admiration, just as Monsieur Mandine had done earlier on.

'What about it? . . .' he asked so as to prevent the silence becoming too awkward.

'Nothing . . . Catherine knows the people that side of the harbour . . . She must surely have heard them talking . . . I'd like you to tell me what they're saying . . .'

48

When Hubert Cardinaud was still going to school one of the other little boys had been at death's door. It was stated he had a temperature of 106°. Then, a few days later, he had returned to school, rather pale and his hair lustreless, and Cardinaud could recall the fascination with which he regarded him, as a being apart, as a boy who had almost died, as if it gave him a permanent superiority over his fellows.

The memory came back to him when he saw Lucien looking at him as he himself had once looked at the boy who had escaped death. It was a comforting thought. If there had been a mirror in the workshop, he would have stolen a furtive glance at his reflection.

It was all right. They had thought he was finished, crushed, and here he was walking amongst people like a ghost. And they were astounded at his calmness, at his self-possession! It was he who was attacking them!

'You know these sort of stories better than I . . .'

He himself had left the district; he had deserted that world where everyone knows everyone else and stories about one and all are freely circulated.

'Where's Titine's son been these past few years?'

'He's supposed to have been in Africa . . . He joined up in one of the Colonial regiments . . . After a bit he got fed up and left the army . . . Some people say they met him in the Gaboon . . .'

'Has he been back long?'

'Ten days or so . . . He came off the *Aquitaine,* that's the boat that's been unloading timber by the warehouse wharf, at Tinant's . . . Won't you really sit down? . . . Cigarette?'

Lucien was rolling one and that too, for his brother, was a mark of vulgarity. People passed now and then in the sun-soaked street, people going up onto the Remblai, on their way to the beach. On the floor, amongst the shavings, there was a half-empty bottle of wine with a thick glass tumbler upside-down over its neck.

'I wonder,' Cardinaud was muttering, 'when he got to know Marthe . . .'

'You don't think he . . .?'

'You know perfectly well he did!'

'People will say anything!'

'It's true . . .'

Yes, indeed, it was true! What people had got to realize, once and for all, was that he knew it, that he would never blush in front of them again.

'What have you heard? Don't be afraid to tell me . . .'

'They say he hasn't even been to see his mother, he's not once left his room, he had to send for a doctor . . .'

'What else?'

'Apparently . . . mind you, this is only rumours . . . apparently he had stowed away on board the *Aquitaine*, in the hold . . . There was some sort of a fight . . . He crawled along to the "Green Bar" one night . . . He didn't know his sister was a barmaid there . . . She was only a kid when he'd left home . . . But he used to be one of the clients of the establishment, you see what I mean . . .?'

No! Cardinaud didn't yet see, but not a word was being lost on him. He was registering everything. He was linking words, facts, images to one another.

'Where is the *Aquitaine*?'

'I don't know . . . It's a Delmas and Vieljeux boat, from La Rochelle . . . She's probably gone back to her home port, unless she's sailed again for Africa . . .?'

'What else are they saying?'

'Well, on Sunday Mimile left Les Sables . . .'

'What time?'

'In the evening . . .'

So all the time Cardinaud was going round to his parents, to the Vauquiers, past the cemetery, at the time he was ringing the Herbemonts' doorbell for them to find him someone to look after the children, even when he returned on his bicycle along the seafront, Marthe was still there, quite close to him, and it was only a matter of chance that he hadn't . . .

'When did they get to know each other?'

'I don't know . . .'

'She's never mentioned him to me,' he said gravely, without bitterness, as though he were discussing a matter of little importance.

'You can't help thinking she . . .' Lucien said vaguely.

'Yes, you can't help thinking so . . . Still, it's strange.'

Strange and sad, very sad, sadder than anything else, sadder than the whole drama itself. It explained so many things. Amongst others, something Cardinaud's mother once said.

'Your wife's a nice girl, but she's bloodless, she doesn't get any kick out of life . . .'

A creature one seemed to see through a muslin curtain. She used to do what she had to do. She was thorough. There was never a complaint to make to her. She used to go for walks. She used to take care of the children. She used to cook as well as she could and the house was well run . . . But . . .

It wasn't a question of blood, as Mother Cardinaud thought, but then all thin people were anæmic as far as she was concerned.

'I wonder where they could have gone . . .'

Lucien spoke unthinkingly:

'Not very far, as Mimile can hardly have any money . . .'

It was one detail at least that no one knew, except perhaps Monsieur Mandine: those three thousand francs which Marthe had taken with her!

For not only had she gone to meet Mimile in the sordid 'Green Bar', but she'd taken the money, the housekeeping money, the money for the house!

'Thanks a lot, Lucien . . .'

'What are you going to do? . . . Mother's getting worried about you . . .'

'Why?'

Yes, why be worried about him?

'You ought to go along and see her . . .'

He would go. To show her that he was keeping calm, that there was no need to dramatize the situation.

'*Au revoir*, Lucien . . .'

'*Au revoir*, Hubert . . .'

'Give my love to Catherine and the children . . .'

A hundred yards away, he turned round and saw his brother, with a plane in his hand and the cigarette, which had gone out, in his mouth, watching him as he made his way down the ever-narrowing perspective of the sloping street.

A little later, he was going down the stone steps and into the basement where he had spend his childhood. His mother, with her knees parted wide beneath the blue apron, was podding peas. He kissed her on the forehead, as usual, shifted the cat out of the wicker armchair and sat down in it, and said quietly:

'Marthe's gone off with Mimile . . . Titine's son . . .'

If he had followed his own inclinations, if he hadn't been afraid, half-superstitiously, of defying fate, he would have added just as naturally:

'I'm going to get her back . . .'

And bring her home, where she belonged!

His mother, too, looked at him in the same way as Mademoiselle Trichet and Lucien had done, as if he had just recovered from some illness and had to be looked after.

# CHAPTER FOUR

THIS time he not only sensed Marthe's presence, but he spoke to her. It happened quite ordinarily, in full daylight, in the sunshine, in a setting of exceptional brightness. He was sitting on a varnished pitchpine bench. The walls were a startling white, adorned with brand-new panelling up to half their height. Everything smelt new. More than an hour ago now Cardinaud had walked along the lanes of Monsieur Tinant's timber-yard and turned past stacks of fir planks and hardwood logs to reach the new offices, a building with such an expanse of glass window that it stood there like a railway signal-box.

'Monsieur Tinant won't be long . . .'

Cardinaud could see him through the glass partition. The timber merchant was in busy conversation with Maupi, from the ice-factory. Then, after a few minutes, Maupi shook him by the hand and moved towards the door where his car was waiting outside. Did he turn back again because he noticed Cardinaud? He half sat down on the table, lit a fresh cigarette, pushed his pearl-grey hat to the back of his head.

Cardinaud had now been waiting more than an hour. Behind another partition, some typists were tapping away at their machines. Elsewhere was the rhythmic noise of a circular saw, and you could see the harbour's edge and the mooring bollards to which the *Aquitaine*'s hawsers had probably been made fast.

That was all. It was hot, very hot. Monsieur Tinant, who was occasionally glancing at him, was a good-looking man in a light suit and he was the owner of a magnificent villa under the pines. There were stories of Monsieur Maupi's sometimes gambling till six in the morning at the casino.

Cardinaud was just sitting there waiting, and here he was, at a certain moment, suddenly saying, in a very low voice, admittedly, and scarcely moving his lips at all, but perfectly clearly, as if he were talking to somebody:

'You see what you've done to me?'

He was talking to Marthe. He was looking at the berth the *Aquitaine* had occupied, and then at the office in which the two men had talked about him and were perhaps still talking about him. Maupi had changed his mind just as he was leaving. The reason he had turned back was surely to say:

'By the way, you know what's happened to that poor boy outside your office?'

Not that they minded about keeping him waiting. They were taking their time chatting of this or that. Once again Maupi walked over to the door, changed his mind, and then at last, after an hour and a half, went out and started his car.

'Come in, Monsieur . . . Monsieur Mandinaud, isn't it?'

Monsieur Tinant was confusing or pretending to confuse the two names. It was the firm of Mandine which handled all his insurance. It was Cardinaud who dealt with him directly. The timber merchant made one name out of the two.

'Cardinaud . . .' the junior member of the firm corrected. 'I'm sorry to trouble you . . .'

Why was Monsieur Tinant behaving so circumspectly and pretending to be on the point of leaving?

'I can only spare you a few minutes . . . If it's to arrange an insurance policy, it would be simpler for you to see my accountant . . .'

'It's not to arrange a policy,' Cardinaud replied quietly.

'Oh! . . . In that case . . .'

'I wanted to ask you, Monsieur Tinant, if you know anything about the *Aquitaine* and what happened . . .'

The merchant rose, walked up and down the office, with his thumbs in the armholes of his waistcoat.

'Look here, Monsieur Cardinaud . . . I've got it right this time, haven't I? . . . I know nothing of what happened and I've good reason to think that nothing did happen, and if your firm has got hold of this business, all I can say is that, as far as I'm concerned, I'm covered . . .'

Cardinaud had been frowning, then he suddenly realized, and he was half inclined to smile, a heartbroken smile.

'I'm not here on behalf of the firm, Monsieur Tinant . . .'

The timber merchant was not yet wholly reassured.

'Even if the accident did take place on your wharves . . .'

How could he explain what he felt? Monsieur Mandine had refused him three thousand francs, because he didn't know, then when he did know, he had presented them with a sort of secret joy! At the 'Green Bar' they must have gone on making jokes about him hours after his departure and he had sensed only a rather chilly curiosity even in his brother Lucien.

They were all wondering:

'What's he going to do?'

They looked at him with interest:

'Well! So that's what a man's like when his wife's gone off with another man . . .'

Monsieur Tinant, though, was worried about financial complications.

'I'm afraid it's on a personal matter that I've come to bother you . . .'

In that case, it was of no further concern and Monsieur Tinant was already looking for his hat.

'Oh well, Monsieur Cardinaud, I can only say again that I don't know anything . . . I did vaguely hear some sort of story, some story about a stowaway and a fist-fight . . . These are matters I don't have time to concern myself with . . .'

'I'd have liked to know whether it's true that this man . . .'

Monsieur Tinant was astounded.

'Do you want to find them again?'

Strange, obviously! A shrug of the shoulders.

'It's your own affair . . . Go and see my foreman, you'll find him on the quay . . . The *Aquitaine* unloaded some undressed timber from the Gaboon on my wharves, that's all I want to know about it . . . I only ask you not to hang around on the wharves and not to interrupt the work in progress . . .'

As he went out, hat in hand, and as he returned again into the quivering sunshine, Cardinaud was repeating under his breath:

'You see!'

'You see what you've done, Marthe?'

A phrase came to mind, a phrase from church that brought with it organ-music and incense: . . . *the cup to the bitter lees* . . .

And calmly, simply, with his hat in his hand, he was making inquiries of the foreman.

'Was it the boss who told you to . . . ?'

An anxious glance towards the glassed-in offices, as if to make sure that it was really all right with the boss.

'I can't be positive about it, but as a matter of fact I was told that it was Titine's son . . . The boat had lain out in the roads until eleven at night, waiting for the tide before entering the harbour . . . A fortnight ago it was, thirteen days to be precise . . . I'd gone aboard to take a look around . . . Just as I was crossing the gangway, I heard a noise on deck, voices, a scuffle . . . I was with the skipper . . .

' "What's going on?" he called out in the darkness.

'Silence . . . Then a dull thud, a groan on the quay-side . . . Then a voice, not far from us, saying:

' "It's nothing, Captain . . ."

' "What were you doing, Drouin?"

'And the second engineer, a fellow a couple of heads taller than me, grunted:

' "Just a rat I chucked overboard . . . I'll tell you all about it in a minute, Captain . . ."

'We went on shore . . . We made a search with a torch and found traces of blood on some of the stones . . .

'It wasn't till a couple of days later that I heard about Titine's son hiding out somewhere near St. Nicholas's Church . . . In a *bistro* where his sister's working, apparently.'

All of a sudden, as he watched Cardinaud, the foreman seemed to understand and looked embarrassed.

'That's all I know . . . I've got to supervise this load, now . . .'

He was touching his cap . . .

'You see, Marthe? . . . This wharf all sticky in the sunshine . . . That's where the boat was, like a black wall . . .

'And now here's your husband taking a perfectly ordinary look around. He just wants to understand, to go over the whole thing from the start. He takes a few paces. He stops. He stares at some stones, perhaps the ones that had blood on them, then at the fence round the timber-yard, and the swing-gate which the injured man, crawling along like an animal, pushed open . . .'

Actually, the foreman did not smile, had no trace of mockery in his voice nor in his expression, but by the end he was plainly being more cautious, since he wondered if it wasn't something that might get him into trouble. As far as he is concerned, it isn't Cardinaud who matters, it isn't the cuckold, it's this fellow they toppled overboard onto a wharf that he's responsible for . . .

Cardinaud returns home. The life of the town hems him

57

in on every side. It's no good trying to think; he meets people, greets them, hears the familiar noises, unconsciously gazes at the blue-sailed sloops returning to harbour, glances from a distance at the loathsome green building where a girl, whom he'll know from now on, is wiping the sticky table-tops.

Mademoiselle Julienne is in his house and Mademoiselle Trichet has asked her into the drawing-room.

'I hope you don't mind my calling, Monsieur Cardinaud . . . I thought I'd come and say hello to the children and bring Jean some sweets . . .'

Mademoiselle Trichet has glanced at her wrist-watch and must have noticed that as it was not yet a quarter-past twelve, Cardinaud can't have come from his office.

Her cooking is not like Marthe's, with the result that the meals give him rather the impression of eating at a restaurant.

'If I don't get back this evening, mademoiselle, do you mind if I ask you to stay the night in the house?'

'Certainly, sir . . . If you'll just allow me to go and telephone to my mother, so she can bring me my things for the night . . .'

Those words . . . A strange picture . . . She'll be undressing in the bedroom, sleeping in the double bed . . . There isn't another one in the house . . .

At one-forty he catches the train. People who don't know, in the compartment, look at him perfectly ordinarily and a girl asks him to shut the window, because of the dust.

He changes at Luçon, waits a long time on the platform, finally gets out at La Rochelle.

He is like a stubborn ant, stubbornly pursuing its path towards its destination, and every time it drops its load, it picks it up again, though this load is much larger than itself.

He goes into the offices of Delmas and Veiljeux. If he

is forced to explain everything, he will explain. In the gloom of a majestic hall, he leans forward across a counter.

'The *Aquitaine* . . . At the moment she's refitting, at La Pallice . . .'

'You don't know where I could find the second engineer, Monsieur Drouin?'

A ledger. Names and addresses.

'He lives at Lauzières . . .'

'Thank you very much . . .'

'You see, Marthe?' It is hot. And yet he doesn't think of having a drink.

'Excuse me, constable . . . Lauzières, please . . .?'

For almost an hour he waits for a bus at the corner of the Quai Vallin. He gets out at Nieul. The driver kindly directs him.

'Go on past the cement works and keep straight ahead . . .'

So he tramps a couples of miles along a powdery road till it leads him to a white village beyond which spreads, like a backcloth, the boundless mother-of-pearl sea.

'Drouin? . . . Which one? . . . The oyster man? . . . Or the sailor on the Delmas boats? . . .'

He has the sudden feeling that his journey has already been a long one and that the way ahead of him is still interminable. A low house, set to one side. He knocks. No one answers. He knocks again, and a window opens in the house opposite, a fat woman with a drooping bosom tells him:

'They're both in the garden . . . You can go through the gate . . .'

An untidy shrubbery. Some vegetable beds, well-kept paths, flowers noisy with bees . . .

A man, down at the end, by a shed, sees him approach: this is the fellow two heads taller than the foreman at Tinant's. A woman, stooping down, is transplanting lettuces, in spite of the heat . . .

The man says nothing and goes on watching this stranger in the black suit coming towards him and greeting him politely.

'Monsieur Drouin?'

'Yes. What is it?'

'Excuse me disturbing you . . .'

He's always excusing himself. Isn't he right to do so, since he is inflicting his own private drama like this on everybody, on people he doesn't know, to whom he means nothing?

'I just wanted a few words with you . . .'

Drouin was working on his rabbit-hutches. He acquiesces and moves towards the house, showing the way. He opens a door, goes through the kitchen, and ushers the stranger into a little parlour with a writing-desk and a great many photographs. The shutters are closed. The room smells of jam. Some clotted cream is dripping in a muslin bag.

'I've called to ask you, Monsieur Drouin, what you know about the man . . . You see what I mean . . . I'm from Les Sables . . .'

Drouin has a big nose, big features and big eyes of very soft blue. He has asked his visitor to sit down and remains standing himself; he looks Cardinaud full in the face, frankly, giving him his full attention.

He is waiting. He knows the visitor will have to explain things.

'You see, Marthe? . . . It's got to be done . . . *to the bitter lees* . . .'

'I am young Cardinaud . . . On Sunday my wife went off, she went off with the man you . . .'

He would have liked to smile, humbly, by way of apology. The other man stands stock-still like a marble statue.

'. . . I believe it's a lad I know, who used to live in Les Sables; I even went to school with him . . .'

His voice sounds slightly thick. A hay wain goes past

60

down the narrow road and the load of hay brushes against the walls and the shutters.

Cardinaud feels he can understand what this colossus's weighty stare implies.

'I want to get her back . . .'

Embarrassed by Drouin's silence, he is on the point of rising.

'Don't get up . . .'

Drouin opens the cupboard of a sideboard, almost exactly the same as the one at home, at least at his parents' home. The same smell emerges. It is almost the same act that his father goes through, the decanter placed on the table, and the tiny glasses with gold rings. Eventually after they have clinked glasses and their lips have sipped the pale liqueur, Drouin rather reluctantly asks:

'What do you want to do?'

'I've got two children . . .' he answers. 'The baby girl's eight months old . . . I've found a nice person to look after them, for the time being but . . .'

Another reminder of Cardinaud's father, the business of unhooking a pipe from the pipe-rack after rejecting two or three others.

'What about him?'

Cardinaud's eyes open rather wide. He glances to left and right. He spreads the palms of his hands wide . . . As if to say:

'Him? . . . But . . .'

The wide world . . . There's the whole wide world stretching beyond the house in the Avenue de la Gare . . .

Then, at last, Drouin sits down, with the comfortable sigh of a giant allowing himself a rest.

'He's a rat . . .' he says. 'I didn't want to bring the police into it . . . You understand?'

Not very clearly. He can guess. He can guess that men like Drouin need no one else to arrange what is their own affair, even if it's a question of law and order.

61

'Have you been to the Gaboon?'

'No . . . I've hardly ever left Les Sables . . .'

'For twenty years we've been going there three or four times a year, in the old days with the *Jérusalem*, for the past few years with the *Aquitaine* . . .'

There are photographs of these boats on the wall, enlarged and framed like family portraits.

Someone knocks on the shutter. Drouin half opens it.

'In a minute . . .' he says to the man in the straw hat and linen suit, who has probably come to fetch him for a game of *belote* . . .

He closes the shutter again and relights his pipe.

'I've known Chitard for five or six years . . .'

An odd thing! Cardinaud himself, with his home in Les Sables, and having been at school with Emile, never even knew his surname. Chitard! Titine Chitard! For she must have given her own name to her children.

A wave of the hand as if to drive a fly away.

'If you don't know, it would take too long to explain . . . He was a little squirt even then . . . Yes, a squirt . . . You know what I mean? . . . All thin and wiry, nervous, shagged eyes, which always seemed to be looking for somewhere to fasten on . . . We had two or three drinks together . . . He was employed in some firm or other . . . He used to get up to shady deals . . . I told him . . .'

Despite his height and weight, the giant seems to be finding it difficult to construct so vast a world before the eyes of this gentleman . . . what's his name? . . . Cardinaud, yes . . . whose wife . . . and who sits there listening, as serious and well-behaved as if he were at a lecture . . .

He can see it himself . . . He knows it all . . . The long concrete road in Port-Gentil which, at high noon, is like melting steel to step onto . . .

Small-time adventurers, he has known many of them . . . He has seen them arrive and seen them depart, hanging their heads . . .

But Chitard, whom the native women call Chichi—he gave himself this ridiculous name—is really nasty. He gets a giddy thrill out of doing harm, playing a dirty trick, or behaving in a revolting manner . . . He seems to do it on purpose, and then looks at you as if to say:

'You think I'm disgusting, eh? . . . And yet you daren't do anything about it! . . . You put up with me . . .'

Whereupon he feels no shame in flinging himself down on his knees, weeping, beseeching, as he talks about his mother, his miserable background . . .

That's what he did after he had pinched from the cash-box once too often . . . He implored them so much that they sent him off into the jungle . . . He was gone for a spell of two years . . . They began to hope . . . Far from it! When a cargo of timber was being loaded, he was on his way back to Port-Gentil and at it all over again . . .

It seizes him just as marsh-fever seizes its victims, in crises. Nothing can stop him then.

The police themselves are driven desperate by him, but as he is a white man . . .

'If they catch you once more . . .'

He went under, for good. The European quarter is practically barred to him. People pretend not to recognize him. He lives in a native hut, in the native quarter. He prowls around the boats. He fleeces the sailors, procures women or contraband for them, begs from the ship's cooks and they slip him something from the galleys out by way of the scuttle . . .

There is one other man like him, an ex-convict, but he at least has the excuse of being an old lag . . .

Chitard is under thirty!

'You understand, Drouin? . . . You're a decent chap! . . . You must understand what I'm getting at . . . If only some-one would help me, if I could just escape from this cage . . . It is a cage . . . Wherever I go, I seem to bang against the bars . . . But I haven't even a couple of francs in my pocket! . . . I haven't had any meat to eat for weeks . . . I shall starve . . . And all this time my poor mother . . .'

Drouin is not taken in. Time and time again, he gave him a little money and it did no good at all.

'If I have to spend another week in this place, I'd sooner kill myself . . .'

The giant says softly:

'Of course I knew it was only play-acting, but I wanted to give him a last chance . . . I hid him away in the hold . . . I had rigged up a place for him behind some balks of mahogany and okoumé. I had given him provisions . . . Three or four times during the crossing I brought him fresh food and something to drink . . . He was like a dog on a chain . . . He would have licked my hands . . .'

Cardinaud was asking earnestly:

'How long did the voyage last?'

'Three weeks . . . We stopped *en route* . . .'

Drouin can guess what the young fellow from the insurance firm is thinking.

'I've seen others do a harder stint than that . . . And he wasn't much better off in his den in the native quarter . . . We were supposed to unload at Bordeaux . . . In mid-sea, we had orders to make for Dieppe . . . It's always like that! . . . You never know where you'll land up . . . On the last day we got a message giving Les Sables as our destination . . . I didn't then know that Chitard came from Les Sables-d'Olonne . . . Those are the sort of questions you never think of asking, out there . . . We cut the engines some way out as it was low tide . . . We stayed there for hours watching the white line of the beach swarming with tiny black objects . . . In order to gain time, and because I was afraid I might be busy once we were in harbour, I went to fetch Chitard out of the hold and got him through into my cabin without anyone seeing . . .

' "Don't move . . ." I instructed him. "When we're in harbour, I'll come and fetch you . . ."

'I locked him in . . .

'Your health! . . .'

He refilled the tiny glasses with meticulous care.

'You know the procedure . . .'

No. Cardinaud doesn't know, but never mind.

'The pilot came on board to bring us in. We had a drink on the bridge . . . It was nearly eleven by the time we were made fast at the quayside . . . I went below . . . I opened the door . . .

' "We're in Les Sables, aren't we?" he said.

' "Yes. So what?"

' "Nothing . . ."

'He pushed past me like a mangy dog, without a word of thanks . . .

'Well, I don't know what put it into my head. I have a gold watch which my father left me . . . I always used to keep it in a drawer . . . So I opened it . . .

'Then I dashed out into the passage . . . I ran up on deck just as the little bastard was flinging a leg over the rail and letting himself slip down . . .

'I caught him literally by the scruff of the neck. I roared:

' "Hand it over! . . . "

'And he knew what I meant, he was trembling all over, he stuffed his hand into his pocket . . .

'I think I wouldn't have gone any further . . . A wave of anger, like that, and it's all over . . .

'But just at that moment, just as he was going to give me my watch, I saw a nasty look come into his eyes . . . I didn't catch on quick enough . . . With a movement I wasn't expecting, he had already chucked my watch into the harbour . . .

'I didn't lose my temper . . . I hit him, deliberately, full in the face, and his jaw cracked under my fist . . . Some figures were approaching in the darkness . . . In order to avoid questions and complications, to avoid telling the whole of this dirty story, I picked up my little fellow and flung him overboard . . . It was on the side of the quay . . . I never gave a thought to it . . . It was just too bad! . . . Those sort of creatures aren't finished off by a little thing like that and we didn't even find him again . . .'

Cardinaud had gone quite pale and drops of sweat could be seen on his brow. Perhaps, if he had had to stand up straight away, his legs would have folded under him. He waited there, stupefied, the little glass edged with gold in his hand.

Drouin got to his feet and pushed back the two halves of the green shutters, revealing a section of the sunlit road. He added, addressing himself:

'Perhaps I should have smashed him up . . .'

Cardinaud succeeded in placing his glass on the table. Then he stood up, looked round for his hat.

'Thank you very much . . .'

He had scarcely had anything to drink but a thimbleful of Charentes cognac, and yet he was like a drunken man. He bumped against the sideboard.

'Thank you very much . . . I'm so sorry to have . . .'

Drouin's blue eyes were frankly asking:

'What are you going to do, now?'

And Cardinaud was incapable of answering.

'I'm afraid I've disturbed you . . . You were busy . . .'

'I'm just pottering . . . We breed rabbits . . . When I'm on shore . . .'

The dark passage was cooler. The two men should have shaken hands, but Cardinaud forgot to do so.

He felt the villagers were watching him as he went past. The ribbon of road coiled its way across the plain. A postman on a bicycle turned round to look at him. At Nieul he collapsed into a chair, on the terrace of the little café with a red pipe over the door where he had to wait for the bus.

'That's how it is, Marthe! . . .'

He had reached a turning-point, as it were. The road no longer ran straight ahead of him. Like a piece of machinery that has only been set going for a particular task, he had stopped, stupidly.

'You're sure there is another bus, miss?'

'In a quarter of an hour, sir . . .'

'And it connects with the train at Luçon?'

'Oh, I don't know about that . . . You can ask at the station . . . '

He was afraid of staying there. He wanted to be back in Les Sables right away, to enter his house, to see the children again, to . . .

'Aren't you getting out at Luçon?'

'Yes . . .'

'We're there . . . '

'Sorry . . . '

What was he thinking of?

At nine in the evening, when the sun had not yet set, he was getting out of the train at Les Sables station. There was a choral society, on its way back from some celebration, waiting for the train. The men were wearing white trousers and flat gold-braided caps, and several of them looked tipsy. He was worming his way between their ranks, knocking against the instruments in their loose covers, stammering:

'Sorry . . . Sorry . . .'

The avenue . . . His house . . . He had the key in his pocket . . . Supposing Marthe . . . He was trembling at the thought . . . He didn't dare look through the keyhole . . . From the moment he was in the passage he could recognise the smell of home, and a special sort of calm that belonged to his own house . . . He was listening . . . A door was opening, on the first floor . . . A hushed voice:

'Is that you, sir?'

'It's me . . .'

'Don't come upstairs straight away . . . I didn't think you were coming back and I got undressed . . .'

Did she have her hair in pins, like Marthe? Had she already got into the double bed, near the cradle and Jean's cot?

He opened the larder and took a piece of cheese. Then he drank a glass of water from the kitchen tap. Above his head, Mademoiselle Trichet was going to and fro with little mouse-like footsteps. He guessed she was re-making the bed. Eventually she came downstairs, correct and serious as he had always seen her, with a little case in her hand.

'You must have been hot? . . . You've had some dinner, I hope?'

He said yes, anyway.

'Jean had a tummy-ache, but it's nothing serious . . . still, he'd better not have an egg to-morrow morning . . . It's the heat . . .'

Yes . . . yes . . . Many thanks! Thanks a lot! . . . Jean had a tummy-ache because of the heat . . . Was that right! . . . For he had heard the words, but their meaning remained a little confused . . .

'Do you really see, Marthe, tell me, do you really see what you've done, my poor Marthe?'

'Good night, sir . . .'

'Good night, mademoiselle . . .'

The familiar sound of the door.

And then nothing more, only a steaming luminous haze, a trail of melting steel in the centre of Africa, in the centre of the world.

'Do you see?'

# CHAPTER FIVE

Was it Wednesday or Thursday? It was unnerving to be asking oneself so stupid a question.

Monday, Tuesday . . . Days so full, so weighty with the present and the past, that it made him giddy . . .

Sunday . . . Trinity Sunday Mass, when Cardinaud still did not know, the apéritif on the Remblai, the cake from the Dufours, the red string, then suddenly that draught in the house . . . And now Mademoiselle (he was no longer adding Trichet) was already installed beside the children . . .

Monday . . . Monsieur Mandine was refusing him the three thousand francs, because he did not know that his assistant had been deceived by his wife . . .

Tuesday . . . Monsieur Mandine gave him the three thousand francs . . . Monsieur Mandine was calling him his dear friend . . . Monsieur Tinant was suspicious . . . La Rochelle . . . The white road between Nieul and the bright white village of Lauzières, and that other road being conjured up, at Port-Gentil, the mangy hound down in the hold for . . . how many days had Drouin said?

And now Wednesday . . . A Wednesday Cardinaud believed to be finished, a Wednesday so distressing that when he left the bus, at seven o'clock in the evening, in the Place de la Liberté, his legs were ready to drop. Do other people ever look at their own neighbourhood, the one where they have spent all their lives, at their house, at familiar faces, without recognizing them, through sheer fatigue and stupefaction?

Does that happen to people you pass in the street . . . for, after all, it cannot be that Cardinaud is the only one

to live through a drama . . . But of course! There are others
. . . Perhaps this fat woman coming out of the coach with
her baskets . . . Perhaps even the driver . . .

You cannot tell . . . Cardinaud, for instance, looks at
himself in the mirror of the dairy as he goes past and you
could swear it was just the same Cardinaud returning as on
any other evening from his office.

Nevertheless, he is so stiff all over, as if he had been
beaten up, pounded like laundry in the river, that he would
gladly have sat down on the edge of the pavement. It's a
preposterous idea. He has never seen anyone sitting on
the edge of the pavement, apart from children and old
people . . . Ah well, if he didn't keep a modicum of self-
respect . . .

His house is over there and he hasn't the energy to go
in straight away. Never before has he acted in this way. He
is not a man for cafés. Except on Sundays, after High
Mass . . . He takes a seat on the terrace of a bar into which
he has never set foot before, where there is no one else
and he suddenly has a comforting feeling of coolness.

'A bottle of beer?'

Why not?

It's a decent bar, for people who leave the station too
early in the morning, or for those who reach it before
time. The woman behind the bar knows him by sight.

'Here you are, Monsieur Cardinaud . . .'

And he has an inspiration. He asks, disinterestedly:

'My wife didn't come in here this morining, did she?'

'Yes, she did, Monsieur Cardinaud . . .'

'About eleven, wasn't it?'

'That's right . . .'

'She told me she'd been in . . .'

He can well afford the luxury of this little lie, this air of
being in the know. And he does know, after all!

What had put it into his head, as he set out that morning, at a quarter to nine, as if to go to the office, yes,

70

what put it into his head to go down there, by the ceme-tery, and into that house which has always been so alien to him? He would have sworn, beforehand, that it was a mistake, that this step would only lead to painful conse-quences, and yet it was too strong for him.

As if to give him a warning, fate had thrown his brother Arthur across his path.

'Aren't you going to your office? . . . You know, old chap, you oughtn't to get so upset . . .'

Arthur himself never gets upset. He's a cheerful char-acter.

While his wife was in child-bed, he played cards and if she were to die to-morrow, he would still catch himself humming as he does all day long.

The Vauquiers' house, like a lantern, doors and windows wide open. Voices calling out. One of those rows which provide entertainment for the whole neighbourhood, except that the workmen in the yard no longer bother to listen.

Cardinaud goes in despite it. In the corridor, he comes straight up against his father-in-law, whirling out like a thunderbolt, who stops and glares at him with blazing eyes, his moustache bristling like a cat's whiskers.

'What the —— hell are you doing here?'

He looks like a musketeer in drooping plumes and his eyes are swimming.

'If it's *your wife* you've come to look for . . .'

Before 'your wife' he uses the filthiest adjective in his vocabulary and he uses it again to finish with:

'. . . then ask your mother-in-law . . .'

'Your——mother-in-law!

'They're each as rotten as the other! . . .'

He has done. He slams the door. As far as he's con-cerned, it's nothing out of the ordinary, a daily occurrence, and it doesn't prevent his immediately dealing with his workmen.

'Is that you, Hubert?'

71

She is upstairs. The smell of the bedroom even reaches the corridor.

'Wait for me to put something on . . . What's up? . . .'

It can't be helped! It's going from bad to worse and he knows it. He waits. She comes down, still smeared with the day before's make-up.

'You've got some news of Marthe,' she asks.

'No . . . Only I'd like to know . . . When Marthe was a girl . . . it could only have been when I was doing my military service—did she know Titine's son?'

You might almost think he needed, every day, a certain number of blows on the head!

'Titine's son, I couldn't say . . . If she did know him, him or anyone else, she was still too good for you when she got married . . .'

Was that what he came to find? And what he is going to find next? He goes towards the town. Twice, three times, he goes up and down the same way, from the corner of the Rue de la Pie, where he used to live in those days with his parents, as far as the single-storey house of Mademoiselle Maison, the piano teacher.

This was the way, down these streets, that he used to follow Marthe, twice a day, not daring to say a word to her, stopping in front of some shop-window or other whenever she stopped.

He was still under sixteen when he decided:

'She's the one I'll love all my life . . .'

Because she was aloof? Because she walked along without looking at anyone? Because she looked like the Virgin on the left in the second side-chapel at Notre-Dame de Bon Port?

He never wondered how he was going to make her acquaintance, nor how they would become sufficiently linked to each other to make a couple, and yet it did happen.

Marthe is much younger than he. When he left to do his

72

military service, at Montpellier, she was sixteen and he had still not spoken to her except to stammer, as he let her go ahead of him, on the way into a shop, for instance:

'Sorry, mademoiselle . . .'

And then there are the edelweiss . . . A day has been organized throughout the whole of France for the benefit of children with tuberculosis . . . Edelweiss are being sold in the street . . . He is one of the sellers . . . He wears a blue armband . . . Marthe is selling them too . . . She has grown thinner, her face has lengthened . . . It's a broiling day, since they chose August 15th for it . . . There isn't a single empty space on the café terraces . . . He speaks to her . . .

'I expect you're hot, aren't you, mademoiselle?'

'I'm terribly thirsty . . .'

'Will you let me . . .'

They almost get lost in the jostling round the bar counter. You just have to grab at the glasses of lemonade or beer as best you may . . . Suddenly the crowd squashes them together and Cardinaud, pressed close despite himself to this body he honours, is aware of the most violent emotion of his life . . .

'Sorry . . . I beg your pardon . . .'

The streets have not changed. It is just as hot now. The Italian is selling ices, trundling his yellow cart with two scenes painted upon it: the Bay of Naples and the Eruption of Vesuvius.

It is almost midday. He will have to go home. He tries to imagine Titine's son, Chitard, as the second engineer called him, at the bottom of his hold, down amongst the mahogany tree-trunks.

As he enters his house he has no feeling of sudden shock, which only goes to show that men lack a sense which animals possess. What does strike him is that the smell is no longer the same as it used to be when Marthe was there, since Mademoiselle cooks in a different way. It is enough to create a foreign atmosphere around him . . .

73

'Good morning, Jean . . .'

Jean opens his mouth to speak, Mademoiselle forestalls him.

'Madame has called . . .'

He is about to dash past them, but they stop him.

'She left again, barely ten minutes ago . . .'

And like a fool he has been away at his parents-in-law's, then traipsing round the streets, cherishing his memories! She was here! She went past the coat-rack and her reflection was caught in the diamond-shaped mirror; he looks for it there, despite himself, as if mirrors could retain reflections of faces like a photograph album . . . !

'Did she leave any message?'

'She needed some identity papers and a few odd things . . . She took the green suitcase with her . . .'

'Mummy's been . . .' Jean repeats and Mademoiselle gives him a little nudge to make him keep quiet. 'She's brought me some sweets . . .'

'Which way did she go? . . .'

'She went towards the Place de la Liberté . . .'

Only ten minutes ago! He might have passed her, for he too has come by way of the Place de la Liberté! He dashes out. If she hasn't gone in the direction of the station, she has probably taken a bus. Perhaps . . .

He walks. He runs. The door, behind him, stays open and Mademoiselle's eyes follow him as she holds the little boy back from going down onto the pavement.

There are a dozen or so buses, going in all directions. One of them moves out from the group at the bus stop and cuts across a corner. Cardinaud, walking in the middle of the road, scarcely has time to move out of the way. He stares at the windows as they file past, a little higher than his head, and the miracle occurs, Marthe is there, a rather pale face, two eyes gazing at him, recognizing him, but expressing no emotion whatever.

It is too late to catch the moving vehicle. He dashes towards a bus company official.

'Excuse me, monsieur . . . Which is the bus that's just left?'

The official turns round. How can he tell one bus from another when they are all painted the same beige colour?

'La Roche-sur-Yon . . .' he announces.

At a distance, Mademoiselle, leaning forward, can still see him. And that spoils the whole thing. A large car was coming past, with only one man inside. He wanted to raise an arm to stop him. He could have given any sort of explanation. The car was on its way toward La Roche, too, so . . .

He did not dare, with Mademoiselle looking on. He flounders.

'When is there another bus?'

'In . . . wait a minute . . . in half an hour, yes . . .'

He has a good mind to take a taxi, but there isn't one anywhere in sight. Besides it goes against the grain. There are some things a man like him cannot bring himself to say.

'Fifty francs if you catch up the bus for La Roche . . .'

He is still the son of Cardinaud the Basketmaker, the son of the Breton woman who came to work at the sardine market, still, after all, Monsieur Mandine's employee. Which is why he goes and warns Mademoiselle that he'll not be coming back, then returns to buy his ticket, and is one of the first to take his seat in the bus which does not leave for another twenty minutes.

The sky is slightly overcast. It is a very still and peaceful evening and the *patronne*, behind him, in the fragrant peace of her bar where she sits reading the weekly paper, dares not say another word to him.

So Marthe has been in here. She came into this very bar to watch the house. At that time Mademoiselle must have been doing the rooms and the windows were open, the bedclothes and the pillows on the window-sill . . .

Perhaps she asked:

'Do you know if my husband has gone to his office . . .?'

She will have been told:

'Oh, yes, madame . . . Shortly before nine o'clock . . .'

He doesn't care what they think of her. She went across the street. She must have rung the bell—or else rattled the letter-box—since she didn't take the key with her. She gave Jean a kiss. She brought him some sweets, like a relative or a friend on a visit. She bent over the cradle. She asked Mademoiselle, looking at her curiously:

'Are the children being good?'

Mademoiselle, as Cardinaud would expect, remained very much on her dignity.

'Oh, yes, madame . . .'

'Monsieur isn't too upset?'

'Oh, no, madame . . .'

She went upstairs. She took her identity papers out of the big wallet from which she has already taken the three thousand francs. Then she packed her underwear and dresses into the suitcase, not forgetting the shoes which they bought together hardly a fortnight ago, for now is the time of year one refits one's entire wardrobe.

'Where are you going, Mummy?'

'Nowhere, love . . .'

Cardinaud would have liked to order another bottle of beer. It does him good, but he dare not. They would take him for a regular tippler!

Cornfields, all along the side of the road. A copse or two. A few children in front of the farms and cottages. They stopped three times.

At La Roche, he glances round him as if expecting to catch sight of Marthe.

'Excuse me, monsieur . . . The bus from Les Sables which came in before ours . . .'

They point it out to him where it stands empty, with pink tickets on the floor.

'You don't know where I can find the conductor?'

A wave of the arm towards a little restaurant, all warm with smells, all pulsing with human voices. Appetites grow keener, bodies sweat, elbows spread across the bare tables.

'A lady with a suitcase . . . A young lady, wasn't it? . . . Yes, I did see her . . .'

'You don't know which way she went?'

'She didn't come as far as La Roche . . . Wait . . . Now where did she get out? . . . Ah, yes, at La Mothe-Achard . . . I remember because someone took her suitcase, a red-headed chap I've met before somewhere or other . . .'

He has an hour to wait. He dares not have lunch in this *bistro* where life spreads itself with so much exuberance. He takes a walk around the vast Place Napoléon, which is like a sheet of light and heat, a burning lake on which no one dare set out. He buys a sandwich. He nibbles at it cautiously, keeping it out of sight.

At La-Mothe-Achard, outside the inn where the proprietress is standing at her doorway, he is seized with such a sudden panic that he wonders whether to get out of the bus.

'La Mothe!' the conductor calls to him, the same one who gave Marthe her ticket.

The woman of the inn moves aside.

'If you're wanting a bedroom . . .'

They are not in the hall, but perhaps they are upstairs, and the word 'bedroom' has made Cardinaud blush.

'Can you tell me, madame . . . A little while ago, a young woman with a suitcase arrived on the bus and . . .'

'I see what you mean . . . They've gone . . . Are they friends of yours? . . . What can I get you to drink?'

'Anything you like . . .'

'Have you had your lunch?'

He says 'yes'. It's of no importance. He is no longer

77

hungry. He has a glass of Mareuil wine served in a carafe.

'They didn't tell you where they were going?'

'Wait a second . . . When the lady got back . . .'

So she had been there already.

'. . . they had a snack, at this table, here! . . . They were waiting for a car . . . A sort of taxi I've seen go past here before . . . The car came from Les Sables . . . I remember the young man shook the driver's hand and spoke to him like an old friend . . . As for telling you which way they went . . . It's bad luck missing them so closely! . . .'

He has to wait for the next bus. In the yard where the hens are clucking, an old woman and a young girl are shredding beans. Currants show blood-red amongst the thorny bushes and the flies are buzzing, the cars following one another in a sort of noisy breathing rhythm, along the main road.

Monday . . . Tuesday . . . Wednesday . . .

Some words come into his head, which he automatically applies to his own plight: *first, second, third day of the Passion* . . . Because all his memories, apart from the time of his military service, are connected with church, with one church in particular, Notre-Dame de Bon Port, because the year is broken up by religious festivals, sermons, special rites . . .

*. . . Jesus falls for the first time . . . Jesus falls for . . .*

He simply must get to his feet, cross the road, return home. He would like to go straight to bed but he will have to wait till Mademoiselle has given the baby its last feed and put everything away.

'How much do I owe you, madame?'

'One franc fifty, Monsieur Cardinaud . . . Are you pleased with the governess? . . . She's a very grand-looking person . . .'

He unlocks the door. Another door, the dining-room one, opens.

'Someone's been waiting for you for over an hour . . .'

78

He is on the point of going into the drawing-room, think-ing they are in there . . .

'No, he's out in the yard . . .'

Mademoiselle has a mysterious, slightly frightened look about her.

'In the yard?'

'It was his idea . . . He asked me for some wine . . .'

Cardinaud goes out through the kitchen. He does not recognize the little old man sitting on a chair, with a bottle of wine placed beside him on the ground. The man rises to his feet.

'Ah, there you are, Cardinaud . . .'

He holds out a dark-tanned hand, trembling almost fever-ishly, and Cardinaud realizes that he is half-drunk. He collapses sideways across the chair again, seizes the bottle, and drinks straight from its mouth.

'This person here . . . it must be the maid . . . she was all nice manners about giving me a drink . . . I told her straight, I do it like this . . . Heavens above, you do look hot . . .'

Cardinaud's shirt is soaking.

'Won't you come inside?'

'No thanks . . . You suffocate in these little cots . . .'

Cardinaud casts a nervous glance towards the low lime-washed walls which separate the yard and the little garden from the neighbours' gardens. The Herbemonts may well be in theirs, which is the largest in the street, taking the fresh air. At this time of day voices carry, particularly the hoarse voice of the old man who looks almost like a tramp. He spits on the ground, belches, drinks, snuffles, behaves on purpose in as coarse a way as possible.

'Have you found them?'

'I don't know what . . .'

Thereupon, as if the one word should explain everything, the man introduces himself:

'Dédé . . . !'

Since he appears not to have been understood, he goes on emphatically:

'Ten years' hard labour, twenty years on top of that . . . Dédé of Port-Gentil, what! . . . Didn't Drouin tell you anything?'

These low walls, these gardens surrounding them, these peaceful families taking the fresh air, probably listening to them. Cardinaud feels that it is he who is defiling his street, that he will be held responsible for it all.

'Look here, I got to Lauzières less than half an hour after you left . . . I had a chat with Drouin, he can't help himself, but at least he's a man . . .'

The blinds are lowered on the first floor. It's Mademoiselle putting the children to bed. Cardinaud would have sworn that a thin blue smoke was curling up over the wall, the smoke from Monsieur Herbemont's pipe.

'All I want to say is that it's not your job to deal with that ruddy Chitard . . . He'll get what's coming to him, trust Dédé, even if I have to go back out there as a lifer, even if my head has to tumble in the sawdust . . . What I don't understand is . . .'

If he didn't do it on purpose, if he paid just a scrap more attention to his appearance, he would pass unnoticed in the street. He looks the house up and down, the kitchen neat and tidy, the feeding-bottles which can be seen through the window . . .

'No! . . . What your wife . . . Anyhow, that's her concern . . . She can mind her own business . . . Have you found them again? . . . Drouin told me . . . Because Drouin knows me, of course . . . He knows that once Dédé gets an idea into his head . . . And he's not the sort of chap to give me any of that clap-trap, he'd never tell me:

' "Dédé, don't do this . . . Dédé, don't do that . . ."

'You see, you can meet all sorts of them, even the dirtiest of 'em, and yet there's never been a rat like that Chitard . . .

'Your health! . . . No? . . . As you please . . . So far as

80

Chitard's concerned, you can set your mind at rest . . . The woman, well, it's no concern of mine . . . That's your affair . . . I'll take charge of him . . . And wherever he's hiding out, he'll show a funny sort of mug when he sees old Dédé arrive . . .

'He'll understand, I promise you! . . . He'll drop down on his knees, like he's done so many times before . . . Only, this time . . .

'When I think that out there he slipped between my fingers like an eel . . . I blamed Drouin for that . . . I wonder now whether Drouin knew the truth . . .

'The truth, well, I'll tell you . . . Give me another bottle first . . . Don't be scared! . . . I've never caused scandal . . . You can slip me a thousand francs when it's all over, because I'm broke to the wide . . . It's not a sum that'll make much of a hole in the pocket of a man like you . . .'

Another sulky glance at the house and Cardinaud gets the impression that this sulkiness comes from envy, that it conceals a longing for a life like his, that the old fellow in front of him would give anything in the world to be in his shoes, with or without a wife, whether cuckolded or not.

'That's the way! You're not so finicky as the maid . . .'

If Mademoiselle hears the word 'maid' . . .

'I'll tell you what he did to me . . .'

'Don't talk so loud . . .' Cardinaud whispers.

The man understands, looks at the garden walls, spits in front of him and shrugs his shoulders. For a few minutes, however, he speaks in a lower voice.

'There were the two of us, at Port-Gentil, him and me . . . You know what I mean? . . . Two of us that those gentlemen took no notice of, pretended not to know . . . Only, in my case, it was all past history, and everyone knew that since then I'd been going straight . . . I used to do some good turns and there were some of those gentlemen who weren't above coming to see me on the sly . . .

'But he was a nasty lot . . . Not that it stopped us meeting . . . I used to have a drink with him sometimes . . . Once when we'd had a lot to drink I stupidly blabbed a bit too much . . .

'Drouin knows the whole story now . . . You may as well know it too . . . It doesn't matter what I did at Courbevoie, Courbevoie it was . . .'

An odd thing! His voice grew suddenly softer as if he were speaking of a lost paradise.

'I did time for it, didn't I? . . . I even claim I did time for two of us . . . That's what I told this rat . . . I told him that I took all the blame myself for the sake of my brother . . . That, strictly speaking, my brother should have been out there with me . . . But since he's been running a *bistro* at Carcassonne, he hasn't even written to me any more . . . I don't blame him . . . That's to say . . . It would be too complicated to explain it all to you . . . For a brother, it's pretty rich, I must say . . . As soon as I'd done my time . . .

'Well, anyway, as I told Drouin, who's a white man, this little wretch took advantage of what I'd said to send an anonymous letter . . . and to the Carcassonne magistrate's court too! . . . As it's not quite thirty years ago, those gentlemen sent for my brother, and they haven't left him in peace ever since . . .

'They must get at the truth, that's their line! . . . Never mind the fact that he's got kids, and a job, and that the whole business wasn't for the sake of . . .'

The window on the first floor half opens. Mademoiselle makes a sign, begs them to talk more quietly, because of Jean who has already been over-excited during the day and cannot get to sleep, continually asking who is the gentleman talking so loudly.

'Now do you see ? . . . I'll just add one thing to the good, which proves there are some people who think well of me

. . . The police chief at Port-Gentil sent for me and told me straight, man to man, off the record:

' "Dédé, someone's played a dirty trick on you . . ."

' "It must be Chitard," I replied.

'And he spilt the whole story, as he'd had the papers from Carcassonne.

'I'm not one to mince words and there are some people you can talk tough to . . .

' "I'll do him in," is what I told him.

'And he answered, lighting his pipe:

' "That's no concern of mine . . ."

'You see? Only, the rat got the wind up right away. I searched for Chitard for a week. I know all the houses, all the huts, all the hide-outs . . . I still don't know where the creature ran to earth, green with fright, frightened of old man Dédé, but he managed to clear out, thanks to Drouin who let himself get taken in by his sham-talk . . .

'Then I swore to myself:

' "Dédé, if you're a man . . ."

'And I caught the ordinary ship because I did have some savings and it's common knowledge that, since my time, I've nothing to be ashamed of . . .

'I went to Bordeaux. I made inquiries about the *Aquitaine* . . . Yesterday I reached La Pallice and they mentioned Drouin . . .

'Drouin told me this latest filthy trick . . .

They were seated on iron garden chairs, painted green. There's still a broom and a bucket in the corner of the yard, and these suddenly seem like peaceful, hallucinating symbols of a domestic life which Cardinaud is striving to cling on to.

The Herbemonts are enjoying the fresh air on their little terrace, he feels sure, and if they are not talking, it's because they are listening. The shutter of the bar opposite clatters noisily down. The whole length of the sea-front people are walking slowly along one behind the other, as if in file, most of them stopping for a moment in front of the café orchestras, the children pleading:

'I'm thirsty . . .'

Or else:

'I want an ice . . .'

There is a sense of the infinite and of adventure in the way they gaze at the boats leaving harbour for a night's fishing, boats which before long will be seeing the town as a cluster of stars.

Cardinaud has never left Les Sables except for his military service and almost immediately afterwards he was given a job in the Insurance Company's offices, because of his neat handwriting and his punctiliousness.

He was born here, five hundred yards away as the crow flies, and his parents are probably sitting on their doorstep, his father smoking his long meerschaum pipe.

Yet it is here in his home, in his yard, under the window of Jean's and Denise's room, that two men from the jungle are hunting each other, here that a battle to the death, as savage as a cockfight, is playing out one of its episodes.

Dédé takes a drink and spits. Cardinaud says to himself, overcome by the purity of the air:

'It can't be true . . .'

The little old man will smile, smile just like anyone else, and raise his grinning mask of a face. Chitard . . .

'That's it! . . . Your turn, now . . .'

As if it were Cardinaud's turn to enter the arena!

'I've called on the sister, at the "Green Bar" . . . Folks like me don't take long to discover the right spots . . . I didn't make my little speech to her of course . . . She mentioned you . . . Where are they?'

Cardinaud hesitates. The old man senses it.

'Got to put the cards on the table, eh? . . . Trust me, I'll be straight, and I swear I won't touch the woman . . .'

'I don't know . . .' he stammers. 'I thought they were at La Roche . . .'

'Is that far?'

'Twenty miles . . . But they aren't there . . . I tell you I don't know . . .'

'Is it true you're going to get her back?'

Cardinaud remembers Drouin in his little dining-room, his pondering and then amazed expression. Dédé's expression is slightly more scornful.

'It's your own affair . . . But as far as he's concerned . . .'

He stands up at last. He spits once more. He notices the bottle is not empty and finishes it, putting it to his mouth.

'I'll come round to-morrow to see if you've got anything to tell me . . .'

He chuckles, turns round towards the white wall, and to show he has understood, calls out sarcastically:

'Good night, friends!'

In the passage he bumps against the walls and leans his dirty hands against them. On purpose! Because these walls, kept too clean, are like a slight upon him.

# CHAPTER SIX

IT was the geranium, a perfect, calm, glorious red, that Cardinaud was gazing at, and everything else seemed to exist only for the purpose of modestly surrounding this flower as it was starting its morning life, on a window ledge, stretching its petals.

It was six o'clock. Cardinaud had partly raised the blind of the window, the one that looked onto the yard, and on this liquid morning walls topped with tiles cut across all the little gardens, all the yards of the block of houses, where watering-cans and deck-chairs lay around.

'Pinkie', as she was having her feeding-bottle, with her legs in the air, was trying to catch hold of one of her feet in her hands, and her eyes were following some flickering patches of sunshine on the ceiling.

Jean was still asleep, curled up like a gun-dog, with his hair over his face. The reflections in the mirror over the mantelpiece were as pale as in a water-colour.

Naturally Cardinaud knew there was a geranium on the window ledge. But he had never looked at it before, and now it was from its sumptuous blooming that his thoughts were springing and the temptation born.

There was no one to witness the struggle that was being waged inside himself that morning, in the solitude of the house still half-asleep. His face, which he glanced at several times in the glass, betrayed no sign of his momentary weakening, except perhaps, while he was shaving, a faded, doleful smile.

He had some reason for his tiredness, for the baby had started crying three times during the night and the second time its father had stood for nearly an hour rocking it to sleep.

Why, yes, why shouldn't Cardinaud give up? It was as easy as water flowing down the course it has traced for itself. Everyone was encouraging him to do so, everyone would approve.

He would continue living the same life as in the past, in the house in the Avenue de la Gare, slightly more dour, slightly more melancholy, but that's not so disagreeable. Mademoiselle was there to smooth the corners around him.

He would give a lot of his time to the children, even more than heretofore. He would take them for walks. Marthe had never really liked taking the children for a walk. She looked after them well, to be sure, better than most mothers Cardinaud knew, but without any verve, without any tenderness, and she would never have got down on all fours in the bedroom to make them laugh, nor again would she ever have spent a quarter of an hour just watching them asleep.

He would be both father and mother at once. Everyone would think well of him for it. They would give him a tender, appreciative smile when they met in the street.

'That's the man who was deserted by his wife and who brings up their children so nicely . . .'

Then again practically everything else would go on as before, High Mass on Trinity Sunday would go on, hats being raised, and this inner peace which the memory of the drama would make even more precious.

In his thoughts he was already living this life, with so much vividness that his face was changing, anticipating an expression in harmony with a new frame of mind.

At all ages he had had the privilege, if it is one, of being able to live the part of the character he was going to be. Thus, as a boy, whenever he saw Monsieur Archimbaud's principal clerk going past, he knew already that he would never be a labourer, or a workman, or a shop-keeper, that he would live like the principal clerk, always respectable, with just a fraction of regal stateliness.

Later on, when he was following Marthe about, with her hair still down over her shoulders, he used to live the life of being her husband, in a new house, with children, and the strangest thing was that he had always imagined two children, a boy and a girl.

A key was feeling for the lock, Mademoiselle was coming indoors and bringing in the milk-can. She was going to light the fire. She was grinding the coffee in the squeaking mill.

Mademoiselle Julienne, from next door, would certainly approve if he followed that course and who knows even whether, later on . . .

Jean woke up. Cardinaud helped him to wash his face and get dressed.

'What's Mademoiselle doing?'

The struggle was still going on, Cardinaud was thrusting the temptation from him, really exerting his energy to do so.

If he succumbed, then he would be afraid. Afraid of what? He smirked. He had the urge to give the answer out loud:

'Of the spirit of evil . . .'

And that could be translated as:

'Of disorder . . .'

Of all that crept beneath the harmonious life he used to know, of all that he had just discovered these past few days, of the grating, defiling, sickening malevolence of an anonymous letter, even the paper of which was ugly and the writing loathsomely vulgar, of all that life one could smell—you could smell it like a fetid breath—from inside the 'Green Bar', beyond that terrace with three greasy tables where he had sat . . .

Monsieur Mandine who first refused, then paid up with a smile which Cardinaud could now see again in his mind's

eye . . . Titine's son, in the Gaboon and down in the hold,
Titine's son being struck a blow of the fist in his face and
being flung overboard, falling with a thud of bruised flesh
on to the stone of the quayside and creeping away, covered
with blood . . .

Was Cardinaud really afraid?

Afraid of that reeling Dédé who drank and spat in the
yard, whose every word was a deliberate insult, out of
hatred, or rather out of spite, out of jealousy, hurled at the
calm purity of the neighbourhood?

'Clean your teeth, Jean . . .'

He looked without apparent emotion at the picture still
hanging over the bed, at Marthe's expressionless face, her
head slightly inclined towards his shoulder because the
photographer had suggested it, and he firmly thrust the
temptation from him.

Then he was filled again with the serenity he had always
searched for and had finally acquired. He could look at
himself in the glass with satisfaction.

He would not give up! He would go right to the end
of the tortuous road, with its unknown obstacles, on which
he had set out.

He would go and find Marthe, he would bring her back,
because her place was in the house, near him and her
children; he would go because he did not believe in evil,
or rather because he had faith in the triumph of good over
evil, in the ascendancy of order over disorder, ultimately
faith in a necessary, determined balance in the world.

As she did every morning, when he sat down at the table,
after the ritual 'good morning' and after asking how the
children had slept, Mademoiselle glanced at him inquiringly.

She could not tell what had just been happening. She
believed everything was going on the same, that nothing
had changed, but this much had changed, that from now on
Cardinaud had come to know himself.

When a letter dropped into the box, at the end of the

passage, with its cool tiles, he gave no start and waited till he had finished his breakfast before going to fetch it. The envelope bore Monsieur Mandine's printed heading.

MY DEAR FRIEND,

Would you be so kind as to call in at the office as soon as possible? Many thanks in advance.

Yours sincerely . . .

He had no illusions about it. It was not to give him any good news. As he was prepared for anything, it was with an even pace that he walked towards the Fish Market quayside, greeting the people he knew, the shopkeepers raising their shutters.

He entered the office as if it was an ordinary working day, but he didn't change his coat. He asked no questions of Bourgeois, who was looking embarrassed and had something shifty, something caddish in his manner, as he did when he corrupted one of his girl-friends with stories that were too coarse, or with details that he was probably inventing.

'Come in, Cardinaud . . .'

Monsieur Mandine too was ill at ease.

'No news?'

'No, sir . . .'

'Look here, my boy . . . I've a good deal of work on my hands . . . You asked me for a fortnight's holiday and I gave it you straight away, in view of your particular circumstances . . . Bourgeois should have gone off this Saturday with some friends who have a car . . . Last night he told me that, if he wasn't granted his holiday as arranged, he would sooner resign his job that miss a trip he's been looking forward to for a long time . . .'

Cardinaud said nothing; he already guessed what was coming next.

'Obviously we can't shut the office . . . Bourgeois has his

faults . . . I don't like being spoken to in the tone he uses; all the same, his uncle is one of our important clients and his father has a job in the Préfecture . . . So I thought . . .'

Cardinaud, unexpectedly, made no attempt to help him and his employer looked at him beseechingly in vain.

'Now you are more of a friend than an employee . . . It's possible that one day you'll be in charge here yourself . . .'

Cardinaud knew it was not true, that he had always been tricked by this promise in the same way as a donkey is led on by having a carrot dangled in front of it.

'Only the other day, when you were worried about money, I didn't hesitate to help you, despite my principles . . . Since your inquiries have not led to any conclusion, since they can only serve to make your predicament even more painful, I'm asking whether you'll start work again on Monday morning . . . Look, Cardinaud, I can count on you, can't I? . . .'

'I'll be here, sir . . .'

'Thank you, my friend . . . Of course I knew you'd . . . Apart from that, I gather you've come to a very satisfactory arrangement, that you've found a reliable person to take charge of the children . . . I'm very glad of that . . . You'll see, everything will work out all right . . .'

'Yes, sir . . .'

It was not just a groundless promise he had given. It was Thursday. He was convinced that by Monday the whole thing would be over, restored to order.

Perhaps something would have changed, but no one would notice it. He would no longer breathe the air of this office in quite the same way, he would no longer change his coat and lay his fountain-pen on the table in the morning with quite the same sigh of relief. What was the point of it?

'You haven't any idea of where she's gone?'

'Not yet, sir . . .'

91

'My guess is they'll have got to Paris by now and you know what it's like trying to find someone in Paris . . . Well, I'll see you on Monday, my friend . . . Keep smiling!'

Bourgeois looked as though he were expecting to have his ears boxed, or be heaped with reproaches. Cardinaud merely said to him, without shaking his hand:

'*Au revoir* . . .'

And he picked up his trail where he had left it off the previous evening, without weariness or impatience. As he had to go past his home, he went in for a moment, and sat down in the gloomy cellar-kitchen, beside his mother who asked him:

'Have you got a holiday?'

'Till Monday . . .'

He drank a cup of coffee.

'Father all right?'

'He's gone to buy some osiers . . .'

He went onto the Promenade and walked right to the end of it, as far as the district round La Rudelière. He stopped outside the modern house with 'Family Guest-House' written up and a garage flanking it. He rang the bell. A sickly-looking woman, who was already laying the places in a room where there were several little tables, opened the door to him.

'Léon isn't in?'

'He ought to be on the rank outside the *Hôtel Splendide* . . . Didn't you come along the Remblai . . .?'

'He wasn't there when I went past . . .'

'Then he's taking a fare somewhere, but he always comes back to there . . .'

She was right. Léon was at the wheel of his taxi, opposite a white hotel with a façade that looked like pastry.

'Good morning, Léon . . .'

'Good morning, Cardinaud . . .'

The naughtiest boy in his form, once upon a time. He had subsequently worked as a mechanic. Then he had bought a car on credit and as he could never understand anything in writing, he had come and found Cardinaud to check the documents on his behalf.

By now he had been able to rent a fairly large house and his wife was running it as a family boarding-house; and in the winter they went off to the Midi, she as a cook, he as a chauffeur.

'Can I talk to you for a minute?'

'Come and have a drink . . .'

In the side-street, there was a restaurant which was empty at this time of day.

'What will you have?'

'Anything . . . I want you to help me . . . You must know all the taxis in the town . . .'

'Yes, even the ones that come down from Paris for the season and pinch our customers . . .'

Cardinaud had a curious sensation. It was the first time for two or three days that he had spoken to anyone without their looking at him in a particular way which was a sort of allusion to his misfortune.

'You do know what's happened to me, don't you?'

'What has happened to you? Nothing serious, I hope? . . . At this time of year, you know, we hardly take any notice of what's going on in town . . . Our life's mostly concerned with the visitors . . .'

'My wife's left me . . .'

'Oh!'

Léon lowered his head discreetly, but otherwise was not taken aback.

'You know where she's gone? . . . You want a taxi? . . .'

'No . . . Listen . . .'

He felt no shame, no embarrassment. He did not trouble to see whether the waitress who was perched on a stool behind the counter, rubbing the mirrors down with Spanish white, was listening to him.

'You remember Titine's son?'

93

'Mimile? . . . What's become of that fellow?'

'It's he whom my wife's gone off with . . . I'll tell you . . . Only last Sunday Emile was in hiding at the "Little Green Bar" . . .'

'Isn't his sister a barmaid there? . . . She's a well-known little . . .'

Another word Cardinaud had never used.

'What's he done? . . . Why was he hiding?'

'It'd be too long a story to tell you . . .'

For all that, the question suddenly opened up new horizons. He had been wise to get in touch with Léon. Maybe the man was uneducated. He was still pretty common. But he puts his finger straight away on the facts.

Emile, after the theft of the watch, could not know that Drouin had made no complaint. He imagined the police were on his tracks. He had no money. He had written to Marthe. Someone, probably his sister, had taken the letter to the Avenue de la Gare.

Now the couple had three thousand francs at their disposal. He had first gone to ground in the inn at La Mothe-Achard.

Was it because Chitard's wound was not completely healed, because the bruises on his face were still too plain to see?

'To continue . . . Follow me closely . . . Chitard . . .'

'Who's he?'

'I didn't know his surname either . . . It's him . . . Chitard stayed three days at La Mothe-Achard . . .'

'With your wife?'

'Yes . . .'

'Did you go there?'

'Afterwards . . . They'd just left. That's exactly why I need you . . .'

Léon was rolling a cigarette and trying hard to understand what was expected from him.

'According to the woman who owns the inn, a taxi came from Les Sables to fetch them . . .'

'When's that?'

'Yesterday . . . Wait! . . . From what the woman at the inn said, it was an old crock driven by a bloke in a cap . . .'

Léon began to feel himself on surer ground and was staring fixedly in front of him.

'An old crock . . . A bloke in a cap . . . No . . . Shut up . . . It means something to me . . . First of all, it's not a car belonging to a big garage . . . It's not a taxi from Paris either, or the woman at the inn would have noticed it . . .'

He drank his half-pint and wiped his brown moustache.

'And you're positive Mimile was hiding? . . . In that case, he didn't get onto just anyone, but someone he knew . . . I've got it!'

He stood up and laid a hand on Cardinaud's shoulder.

'You remember Gugusse? . . . The one who nearly bust your leg one night, when he knocked you down on the skating-rink . . . He was a waiter at one time . . . Then he worked on the quaysides . . . Last year, somehow or other, he found an old jalopy, and now he's a taxi-driver . . . Not this side of the harbour, they wouldn't want his machine here . . . At La Chaume . . . He takes the sailors when they're tight . . . And now that you mention it . . . The last time I saw him he was parked a few yards from the "Green Bar", just opposite the Ferry . . .'

And, quite simply, Léon was suggesting, as they moved towards the door, after flinging a handful of change onto the marble table-top:

'Shall I take you? . . . If it turns out he isn't there, I'll be on the spot for finding him again . . .'

On the Promenade, he turned round to the owner of the *Splendide* enjoying a breath of fresh air in his braces.

'If anyone wants me, I'll be here in a quarter of an hour . . . Jump in.'

A moment's hesitation on both sides. Should Cardinaud

get in the taxi as if he were a fare, or next to the driver? Out of tact, he chose the front seat and his friend gave him the credit for it.

'First we'll go and find out whether Gugusse has got back . . . Because if he's gone any distance in that old jalopy of his . . .'

People were recognizing Cardinaud in the front seat of a taxi and were turning round to stare. Léon was driving right round the harbour. They passed not far from Monsieur Tinant's offices and it seemed ages to Cardinaud since he had sat in the glass-enclosed waiting-room. They drew up in front of the Ferry.

'You stay here . . .'

Léon was right. With his badly rolled cigarette between his lips, and his rather vulgar behaviour, he could come up to the 'Green Bar' and be seen joking with Mimile's sister, then going after her into the gloom of the little café.

He was away for nearly a quarter of an hour.

'You should never have come with me . . . The bitch saw you . . . She got the wind up at once and wouldn't talk . . . All I know is that Gugusse came back yesterday evening . . . She maintains she doesn't know where he went . . . He was drinking until one in the morning . . . I don't know where he lives, but I know where he keeps the old bus . . .'

On the other side of the harbour channel, Cardinaud caught sight of the windows of his office and he knew Monsieur Mandine had gone out, since Bourgeois had opened the windows and the smoke of a cigarette could be seen curling up from it.

'At this time of day, you realize, he'll hardly be up . . . He's one of these blokes who only work at night . . . Why, a man I know, a croupier, wanted to keep me parked outside the casino from midnight onwards, to drive home the gamblers, and they, like as not, give you a handful of counters instead of a tip . . . As I told him, I'm a married man, father of a family, and that crowd can . . .'

He spat out of the window, in almost the same way as Dédé had done, the day before, in the yard. Then the car stopped a hundred yards from the Fish Market, at the water's edge.

'Better not let yourself be seen, this time . . . He's supposed to have a room above Lucas the cobbler's . . . You remember old man Lucas?'

He got out and went off towards a side-street, and Cardinaud, embarrassed at sitting there in the front of a stationary car, got out in his turn and went for a stroll.

It wasn't time for the auction. Some railway trucks were on the quayside being loaded with crates of fish while the fish-wives, sitting in the shade of the stalls, were calling their wares and selling their sea-fish.

The sky was becoming slightly overcast. The breeze was blowing sometimes off the sea and sometimes from inland, as if the day were likely to end in a storm.

Cardinaud's eyes fell unthinkingly upon a fishermen's café, beside the Market. He gave a start as he recognized a face and tried to turn away, but he was too late: Dédé had spotted him and was waving a friendly greeting.

The ex-convict was not by himself but sitting at a table with three or four old men and they all looked round, then at once leant across to speak to him.

'You know young Cardinaud?' they must have been saying. 'His wife . . .'

Dédé, standing up, was waving to Cardinaud to come and have a drink with him and Cardinaud didn't know how to refuse, was pretending not to understand. He felt like going away, but the car was there, from which they had seen him getting out; Léon would search for him . . .

Anyway, since he was not making a move, it was Dédé who was making one and coming across the street, hobbling slightly. He reached out a hand.

'How d'you do? . . .'

Then, screwing up his eyes, he looked at the taxi and the side-street down which Léon had disappeared.

'Already on the trail?'

'I'm with a friend . . .' Cardinaud stammered awkwardly.

'I'll be damned! . . . And you don't fancy meeting me here, eh? . . . Don't say no . . . I felt it all right, yesterday evening, that you weren't very keen on the story I was telling you . . . But I'll give you a word of advice, my lad . . . When Dédé's decided to do something or other . . . Dédé's an old dog who doesn't stop at just telling stories . . .'

Changing his tone, becoming almost threatening:

'Where have you sent your mate?'

'I assure you . . .'

He was embarrassed, certainly. The situation was as unpleasant as when one has committed a serious gaffe in society. But he wasn't weakening, nor tempted to do so.

'I shall have to be getting back . . .' he said, glancing at his watch.

'No, you don't! You know very well you've got to wait for your chum . . . Here! We'd better get opposite the end of the street, I'm curious to know which house he comes out of . . . I've already tracked down the mother and the sister . . . I've found out a lot of stories . . . You can't imagine the number of things a man like me, with his eye to keyholes, can find out in a few hours . . . Look! . . . Here's your chum . . .'

Léon was leaving a low house and pausing for a moment as he caught sight of Cardinaud in the company of the old man. He came forward eventually, hesitating.

'How d'you do? . . .' Dédé launched out as he held out his hand. 'I'm a chum of Monsieur Cardinaud's . . . What did they tell you down there?'

With a glance, Cardinaud begged his friend not to talk.

'They didn't tell me anything . . . Why?'

'O.K.! . . . I get it! . . . I'll go there myself! . . .'

And his face looked mischievous again, and just slightly reproachful.

'As you please, my little  lambs . . . It won't stop me doing what I've got to do and there are some who aren't pigeons like you two . . .'

The two men climbed into the taxi again.

'Where are you going now?' asked Léon, grown more sullen.

'I don't know . . . Did you see him? . . .'

'Let's drive on . . . May as well make for the *Splendide* . . . Who was that?'

'Someone who has a grudge against Mimile . . . What did Gugusse say?'

'He was still in bed, with a hang-over . . . He had emptied his pockets onto the table and I spotted a hundred-franc note . . . Straight away he suspected everything . . .

' "Tell me now, Gugusse . . ." I began to say.

'And he came back at once with:

' "I know what brings you here . . . You're a pal of young Cardinaud, the one who won't speak to his school-mates any more and plays so proud just because he's in the insurance . . .

' "But as far as what you want to know is concerned, you'll have to think again . . . That Mimile's a smart lad . . .'

The taxi was stopping in front of the *Splendide*. The two men once more entered the restaurant, where four customers, at half-past ten in the morning, were already playing *belote*.

'Doing well, Léon?'

'Doing fine . . .'

They sat down in the far corner.

'Some beer, Emma . . . Nice and cool . . . I'm fed up, old man . . . I did all I could . . . I told him you weren't what he thought, that Mimile was a rat, that you had two children. He just replied:

'"Go — your grandmother!"'

Such obscenities could no longer affect Cardinaud. He could hear them without flinching. Yet, only a week before, he would have sworn they didn't exist.

Léon himself was surprised, almost shocked out of his composure.

'I wonder how your wife could have . . .'

Exactly! He had to go and find her!

'He didn't conceal the fact that he had driven them somewhere. What time did they leave La Mothe-Achard?'

'About half-past twelve . . .'

Léon was making a mental calculation, moving his lips.

'By six in the evening Gugusse was back, I got that from Titine's daughter . . . If he drove fast, as fast as his old crock can do, he still couldn't have helped stopping at all the *bistros* on the way . . . There and back, he's certainly not done more than a hundred and twenty miles, probably less . . .'

Léon had an urge to shake his former schoolmate and tell him:

'Well, do something, speak, groan, make a guess, don't sit there chewing it over like a cow munching . . .'

He was taking things to heart, perhaps because it had now become a professional matter for him.

'You get it? . . . We know all the sorts of journeys customers may ask to go . . . Suppose they were wanting to go to Paris, or Bordeaux or any large town . . . They'd have no need to take Gugusse's taxi . . . They'd only have to take the bus as far as La Roche . . . There they've got a train in any direction . . . Who is he exactly, that old boy on the quayside?'

'An ex-convict who's come from the Gaboon on purpose to kill Mimile . . . He told me so yesterday . . .'

Decidedly, Léon was growing more and more bewildered.

'So much the better!' he said.

But Cardinaud made no reply and stared at the lace curtains screening the windows of the restaurant.

'I'd say they haven't left the Vendée . . . Why they're staying around here, I don't know . . . I hardly know your wife by sight . . . As for Mimile, I last saw him a good twelve years ago . . . But if I were in their shoes . . . Let's see! . . . Have they got any money?'

'Three thousand francs . . .'

Léon looked at him askance and understood.

'With three thousand francs, they may already . . . There might be a way, if there's still time . . .'

He was hesitating to suggest it, since he had his job, his wife, his children, and a budget to balance. He used to go to the cinema now and then. Supposing Gugusse were more talkative with the old convict who, for his part, would know how to deal with him . . . He need only watch out for him and follow him . . . Eventually, they would get at the . . .

'Listen, if you like, provided it doesn't take more than a day or two . . .'

Where was Cardinaud? What was he thinking of? His inertia was becoming serious, even embarrassing.

'Assuming, of course, that you really want to get her back . . .'

Cardinaud turned a grave, serene face towards him.

'That's not the way . . .' he said, shaking his head.

That wasn't the way, with vulgar, adventure-story methods, to put things straight again. The thing was happening on a different level, a level on which Léon, decent chap though he was, could not follow him.

He was even wondering if he hadn't been wasting his time. No one could accompany him on the path he was following.

'Thanks, Léon . . .'

He hesitated whether to add:

'What do I owe you?'

But the cab-driver would have resented it.

'Thanks a lot . . . I must think things over . . . You've been very kind . . .'

He didn't think to pay for the drinks. He only noticed it when the waitress already had Léon's money in her hand and he protested in vain.

'I shan't forget . . . Thank you . . .'

He shook his hand, on the pavement, and made off in the opposite direction to the sea-front, while Léon, vexed, was wondering whether Gugusse wasn't right, whether Cardinaud wasn't so haughty that he . . .

# CHAPTER SEVEN

THE coach was floating along the main road and all the heads were bowing and swaying at the same time, to the same side, to left, to right, forwards, backwards; and bosoms, when the waves were rougher, heaved as if under the effect of a hiccough.

The woman opposite Cardinaud had a floppy straw hat, vast and shapeless, such as are on sale in shop-windows where there are crudely painted toys and post-cards. She was wearing a purplish red bathing costume over which she had slipped a white linen skirt.

She was already in the coach when it left Les Sables; at La Roche, Cardinaud had noticed a man without coat or hat on who had been reading since they started, and must be her husband.

As far as Sainte-Hermine, she was out of his line of vision.

Now, as the vehicle was pitching and hurtling along towards Mareuil, she was just opposite him. She had a stubborn little forehead, a large fleshy face, and goggling eyes. A patch of sunburn cut across her neck in the opposite direction from the line of her bathing costume and the rest of her flesh was wax-coloured.

She was looking out of the window. Perhaps she was seeing nothing, just as Cardinaud did not see her, even though he stared at her with eyes sometimes wide open. It was five o'clock. The sky was turning to copper. At times the atmosphere was no longer anything but diffused light and one could not look at the sun. It was hot. Some drops were glistening on her wax-coloured skin, springing up particularly in the curve of her neck, and her breasts could be seen sagging under her bathing costume.

She was wrinkling her brows. They had just passed a pair of yoked oxen. She half turned towards her husband who was reading beside her, regardless of the countryside, the stops, the starts, the comings and goings of the passengers.

'Do you think she'll have the cheek to serve us beans again?''

The thin man, with his shirt-sleeves rolled up, frowned. A silence. Cardinaud was still watching her and perhaps he was suddenly wondering what she was doing here in his world.

A farm . . . A copse . . . A drop down a hill . . .

'Still, the lieutenant's wife was quite right to tell her off like that? . . . If she hadn't done so, I would have done . . . What is it again they call beans around here?'

The husband, without raising his head:

'*Mogettes* . . .'

That was all. The wife was pondering, staring at Cardinaud, without meaning to, without realizing it, and the latter suddenly gave a start, a shiver, an extraordinary look of anguish.

Supposing he were mistaken . . . Or supposing he arrived too late . . . The coach, which was tearing downhill like mad, was still not going fast enough for him and this unhealthy atmosphere of before the storm was increasing the tension of his nerves.

All by himself he had followed, he had chosen his path, and now he was going to learn, in twenty, in fifteen minutes, whether the path was the right one.

Léon had mentioned a hundred-franc note on Gugusse's table . . . The previous night Gugusse had drunk till late in the 'Green Bar' . . .

So Chitard had given him some money . . . Out of the three thousand francs . . .

Drouin too had said that on board he was dressed in rags . . . So he had had to buy some clothes, some shoes . . .

*'If they had wanted to catch the train, they would have gone by coach as far as La Roche . . .'*

And the old taxi had only travelled a hundred and twenty miles at most . . . Sixty there, sixty back . . . probably less . . .

Cardinaud had not returned home to lunch. Mademoiselle would be surprised. It was not done. He would apologize when he returned. Since the morning he had been tossed about in one coach after another and now . . .

He clenched his fists convulsively. He was scared. The storm was about to break, it was already starting, you could hear a rumbling like that of a heavy lorry.

Marthe's voice, guarded as ever, unemphatic, dispassionate:

*'Why don't you ask my Uncle Tesson for them?'*

The woman—they were probably small trades-people from Paris—who had been thinking the whole way about the beans at their boarding-house, was nudging her husband with her elbow, because thoughts were passing curiously like a film across Cardinaud's face, while he was entirely unconscious of it.

What Marthe had suggested asking Uncle Tesson for, several years ago now, was the ten thousand francs he needed to borrow to buy the land for the house.

'He doesn't pay us a visit when he comes to Les Sables!' he had replied.

'He doesn't visit anyone . . . He's not that type . . . All the same he assured me that if we ever needed him . . .'

He was the rich man of the family. He had married Madame Vauquier's sister, in other words Marthe's aunt, who was twenty years younger than he.

He had run a large business, in shoe-leather or cobbler's materials, off the Boulevard Voltaire in Paris. He was gentle, rather deaf, always in a light suit and slippers, with careful movements.

The couple lived on a delightful estate, a mile or so out of Mareuil, on the hill. The three or four times that Cardinaud had been there, he had found the uncle and aunt in the park. The picture was always identical. Mareuil was like a child's toy in new colours, beside the river. White paths climbed the hills and lost themselves in the bright green woods. You pushed open a white wicket-gate on which were written the words 'The Mimosas'. And amongst the roses, near a red-tiled roof, you found, under a parasol, an old gentleman dressed in white, and his wife, Elvire, with her hair in little curls, knitting beside him.

Cardinaud never called him 'Uncle', but 'Monsieur Tesson'. Once he had ventured to speak to him about insurance and Monsieur Tesson had looked at him in a thoughtful way.

'How much premium do you think I would pay on "The Mimosas" and our house at Nice?'

Cardinaud, proud of being able to calculate very quickly, said at once:

'About three thousand francs . . . The third-party risks are almost non-existent, but, on the other hand, there are your collections which . . .'

'You get the first premium as your commission, don't you? For the fifty years I've been in business, I've adopted my own habits and had my own ideas on insurance companies as on other questions. You are Marthe's husband. It would not be fair that you should suffer . . .'

Cardinaud had been embarrassed when Monsieur Tesson had simply handed him, as his by right, a cheque for three thousand francs.

'That comes to the same thing, don't you agree?'

Drops of water were dribbling down the windows of the coach. They seemed to penetrate into a cloud and suddenly

106

hailstones were bouncing on the road and making a noise like a toy drum on the roof of the bus.

A moment later came the deluge. Some horses already soaking wet were going along with heads lowered and the waggoner had a sack over his head.

'Emile . . .'

Cardinaud looked sharply at the husband . . . But no! Of course, it was another Emile . . .

'We'll have to wait till the storm's over at the bar opposite the bus stop . . . We shall be late for dinner . . .'

The husband nodded, without realizing that she was trying discreetly to point Cardinaud out to him.

. . . They had not got enough money, that was the whole point. That's why they had not immediately left the Vendée! That's why they were prowling around, until Marthe had said, as she had once before said to her husband:

'I could ask my Uncle Tesson . . .'

He was roused from his relaxation. Something had just torn past like a whirlwind. Jets of water were splashed up from the road now transformed into a morass. It was an old grey car. He could not be positive. It was a feeling rather than a conviction, but surely the man beside the driver . . .

'Sorry, madame . . .'

He had stepped on her bare feet in the intricate sandals she had bought at Les Sables.

'It's all right . . .'

How many miles to go? . . . If it had really been Dédé, in Gugusse's car, then he was not mistaken, and all on his own, using only his wits . . .

The countryside was unrecognizable. The rain blurred everything. The woman, by now, at each flash of lightning, was gripping the arm of her husband, who none the less continued reading.

He knew so many things that he was never suspected

107

of knowing, things that he made out, even to himself, that he didn't know!

Monsieur Mandine's promises, for example . . .

'Monsieur Mandine's promised me that one day . . .'

He smiled. He pretended to believe that one day he would be his employer's partner.

'Monsieur Mandine's been very nice to me to-day again . . .'

But he knew that on his good days Monsieur Mandine was like that with everybody, though sometimes he would say afterwards:

'What a little sh——! '

And the people of the neighbourhood, the lawyer, the big shopkeepers who greeted Cardinaud each morning!

'A good lad . . . A bit of a fool . . . thinks he's a success . . .'

And Marthe?

She did not love him, she had never loved him, she would never love him. He had always known it. Did it matter? He loved her and that was enough, he was happy that she was his wife, that she lived in his house, that she bore his children . . .

It was so much more simple than people thought!

He was on his feet. He picked his way between the legs of the passengers.

'Sorry, monsieur . . . Sorry, madame . . .'

The last downhill stretch was the one into Mareuil . . . His head turned, in impatience, in agony . . . Over there, to the left, in front of the Green Oak Hotel, it was certainly Gugusse's car which had stopped in the rain.

People were crowding under the dripping awning, in the middle of which a pool of water was forming. The town was unrecognizable. Everything was soiled and blurred. Outside the bazaar they hadn't had time to bring in the toys, nor the revolving stand for post-cards. A shop-girl with an umbrella was trying to shift them under shelter.

'Sorry, monsieur . . .'

He brushed against the driver's back, trying in vain to open the automatic door before the bus stopped.

'One minute, please . . . Ticket . . .'

He searched for it in all his pockets, then dashed out into the pouring rain, the thunder and lightning, and found himself in the cool, damp calm of a restaurant.

The coach was emptying and behind him everyone else was coming into the room where their footsteps made dark marks on the floor. The woman in the red bathing dress was looking at him as if to say:

'Here he is again, that chap! . . .'

You might think they had been pursuing him from Les Sables.

'Is there a telephone here?'

'At the back, second door on the left . . .'

It was the safest way: first make sure that Marthe . . . He prided himself on his memory for numbers . . . Only once, ten years before, he had telephoned Monsieur Tesson, from another restaurant, near the bridge.

'Hello! . . . seventeen, miss, please . . .'

'I'll check up that the line's working . . .'

Crackling. Provided only the telephone wires, in the storm . . .

'Hello . . . Hello . . . seventeen? . . . Is Monsieur Tesson there? . . . That you, Monsieur Tesson? . . .'

His hand was shaking. The telephone-box smelt of wet wool and the receiver was getting clammy.

'This is Cardinaud speaking . . .'

A silence, as if it were a matter of indifference to Monsieur Tesson whether it were Cardinaud or anyone else.

'Tell me . . . Is Marthe at your house?'

Supposing they cut the connection? Supposing the storm suddenly . . .

'Hello, I can't hear . . .'

He was shouting, remembering that his wife's uncle was hard of hearing.

'Oh, it's you, Cardinaud,' a quiet voice at the other end of the line was saying.

'I'm wondering whether Marthe . . . whether my wife is with you . . .'

'What's that you say? . . . You're coming to collect Marthe . . .?'

'Is she with you?'

'Do you want to speak to her? . . . Hold on . . . She's just arrived and gone upstairs with my wife, as she was soaked to the skin . . .'

Tears burst at that moment from Cardinaud's eyes. He no longer knew what to say. The uncle, at the other end of the line, was repeating:

'Hello! . . . Hello! . . . Have we been cut off? . . .'

Was it better this way? What could he have added? He hung up, clumsily. He stared, with haggard eyes, at the woman in the red bathing dress, whom he had almost knocked into as he left the telephone booth.

'What'll you have?' the *patron* was asking, an apéritif bottle in his hand.

He replied yes. A little room was made for him at the counter. He was suddenly wondering whether he hadn't lost his wallet, then found it again.

'How much is that? . . .'

He could see himself in a misted-over mirror, between a couple of bottles, and hardly recognized himself. His anguish, however, only depended now upon a material question, a question of time, of minutes, perhaps of seconds? The muddy water was streaming down the gutters everywhere, the awnings were flapping, sallow faces were flattened against all the windows and he himself was rushing out, catching sight of Dédé's car half-way up the slope.

He must think fast, not make a mistake. They had twice stayed at the 'Green Oak', his wife and he. It was known

110

there that they were relations of Monsieur Tesson's. He could not believe, knowing Marthe, that she would have returned to this hotel with . . .

All these theories, in his mind, were certainties. It had to be so. He had no time to hesitate.

Chitard was mistrustful. He knew Gugusse. He must have made the car stop somewhere, without saying where he was going to stay.

And Cardinaud recalled another remark of Marthe's. Several people were fishing. It was on the banks of the Lay, a couple of miles from Mareuil, near a dam, an old mill turned into a guest-house.

'*Next time*,' she had said, '*we'll come and stay here . . .*'

Ah well, next time . . . Next time was this time, and it wasn't with him . . .

She had arrived the day before . . . Why had she only just now gone to call on her uncle? . . . Was it through fear? . . . Unless perhaps Tesson . . . ? . . . The old couple used sometimes to go to Royan for two days or so . . . Perhaps the Tessons had just returned? . . . They had a large car and the gardener acted as their chauffeur . . .

Cardinaud was no longer aware whether he was treading in the water or on firm ground. His clothes and shoes were drenched. The cool water was running down his face and his spirits were rising, he was leaving the little town, he was following a lane he knew well, he was saying:

'You understand, Marthe . . . It had to be done . . .'

Now and then he was looking back, afraid that Dédé's car might have started up. The lane was climbing, going down hill again. A family was huddled under an oak-tree, and they had put the father's alpaca jacket over one of the children. On the river raindrops were sputtering like a firework.

He must not frighten her. It would be better to go round by the path which came out into the yard of the old mill. There were red-checked cloths on the tables again.

111

And here he was reaching his goal, they were opening a door for him, the kitchen door, a girl who had seen him crossing the yard.

'Well, now! You are a brave one, aren't you? . . .'

He could vaguely discern two or three people waiting for the storm to finish.

'Is it true the waterworks have been struck?'

What? Which? A door stood open. On a wall painted green the notice about drunkenness in public could be seen and a coloured print which hung in all the *bistros* in the district.

Cardinaud came forward and, in the low room with its open beams and disarranged benches, he could see him, at the far end of one of the benches, with his face flattened against one of the little lattice windows.

He wondered if he would be able to speak. He could recognize Mimile and indeed the Mimile he could see was not the Mimile of the deeply-lined features, the warped Mimile of the present day, but the boy whose red hair was always falling across his face. So much so that he said:

'Mimile . . . !'

The man leapt round, like a cat, and got to his feet while his arm moved up as if to ward off blows. His lips were trembling. He was terribly thin, emaciated. His mouth . . .

'What do you want with me . . . ?'

So this was where the long trail ended, where Cardinaud . . . His hand searched mechanically for the back of a chair, found none, and he leant against one of the tables. He had, in the pit of his stomach, the same empty feeling as when one is going to be sick and a phrase was buzzing in his ears:

'*Jesus falls for the third time . . .*'

He was not Jesus, he was hardly anything, just young Cardinaud, but God was his witness that he was doing what he could, doing all that he could, with all his heart, with all his soul, with all the strength of his being.

112

He had to swallow hard before speaking again and his voice was as dry as his throat.

'Dédé's here . . .'

The strangest thing was that Mimile used '*tu*' to him straight away as in the old days.

'What's that you're saying?'

He was mistrustful, snarling. He was scared.

'Dédé . . . From Port-Gentil . . . He's a mile or so from here, with a car . . .'

'It was you who told him, wasn't it? . . .'

Cardinaud still had the courage to shake his head. And Chitard was not daring to approach, cautiously keeping a table between them.

'What did he say? . . .'

'That he . . .'

It was a hard word to utter. Cardinaud was unused to it.

'That he would kill you . . .'

The other, slamming his fists together in a way fit to break them, let fly furiously:

'It's Marthe who's got the money in her bag! . . . I haven't a sou in my pocket, nothing . . . I . . .'

Cardinaud saw the glance he flashed at the till behind the bar.

Had he not made up his mind to see the thing through to the end? He still had, in his wallet, a little less than one thousand francs out of the three thousand Monsieur Mandine had lent him.

Mimile's sharp eyes were following his action, and an expression of vicious triumph was coming over his face.

'Give me . . .'

He literally snapped up the notes as animals in the zoo snap up the food that is flung to them. He was looking at the two doors. He was having to choose.

'As for your wife . . .'

One might have thought that, still like a wild animal, he was going to leap through the window. He was trying to think of something spiteful to do or say. It must have cost him something to depart in this way. He couldn't hit upon anything. Fear was hard at his heels. The distant sound of a car set him trembling and he finally spoke, pitifully:

'. . . Say good-bye to her from Mimile.'

The door opened and did not close again. A sheet of rain blew in and soaked the floor as far as the middle of the room.

'Will you have something to drink?'

Slowly, slowly. Cardinaud turned round and recognized the plump little girl who had opened the kitchen door to him.

'I'm sorry,' he stammered.

Sorry for what? He didn't know. It didn't much matter. He was hot. His suit was steaming. Now the maid was asking:

'What came over him?'

'He's left . . .'

He could sense in her something of the anxious amazement the woman with the waxen complexion had shown. He forced a smile to reassure her.

'A drop of brandy?'

Perhaps Dédé was on his way here? What would he tell him?

'You should take your jacket off, so I can put it to dry in the kitchen . . .'

He was scarcely conscious of doing so.

'Your braces have run . . .'

Some mauve braces which Marthe had bought him not three weeks ago.

Provided only she would understand straight away, as he had understood, for he no longer felt he had the strength to talk. He had collapsed onto the bench and, for the first time in his life, he regretted that there was no back to it for him to lean against.

114

The violence of the rain was lessening. The maid was running to gather up the red-checked tablecloths in the yard. The *patron*, whom Cardinaud had not previously seen and who may well have been in the room during his talk with Mimile, was turning the handle of the awning slightly to make the water that had collected in the hollow of the canvas fall to the ground.

'Shall I lay these tables?'

He paid scant attention to the preparations for dinner. Some clean cloths were spread over the tables, carafes of water, *chopines* of white or red wine, napkins in box-wood rings.

There was a sound of voices in the lane. They came closer.

'I'll go and change the children's clothes first . . .'

It was the family he had noticed on the way under a tree. The woman was urging the two children up a narrow staircase. The man was drinking an apéritif before doing anything else.

'I left our rods out there, past the second bend . . . There'll be time enough later on . . .'

Glance at Cardinaud. Questioning look at the *patron* who made an evasive gesture by way of an answer. And now they could hear other voices, a silhouette outlined itself on the terrace, a woman in a white skirt over a red bathing dress was looking in through the window, catching sight of Cardinaud, turning round and saying something to her husband. Somewhere or other they had borrowed a huge Vendée-style umbrella of blue cloth. They were closing it.

'Aren't you soaked, you others?'

'The hairdresser lent us an umbrella . . .'

And she asked, with a touch of tartness which made clear the business about the beans:

'What's for dinner?'

'Rabbit . . .'

'Isn't Madame Turpin back yet?'

'She went off on a trip with the commander and his young lady . . .'

By going across the road, Cardinaud would have been able to see, above the mill, half-way up the hill, Uncle Tesson's estate.

'Are you intending to have dinner here?'

He nodded in reply.

'Now if you're wanting a room, it won't be so easy . . . Unless the lady with that gentleman who's just left . . .'

'He's left?' called the woman in the bathing costume.

'I don't know . . . He's just gone out . . . This gentleman here would be able to . . .'

'He's left!' Cardinaud confirmed.

'But his lady . . . ?'

The wax-coloured complexion spoke in a low voice to the *patron* and then burst out laughing.

'You coming to change, Emile?'

They set off up the steep stairs. You could hear them walking right overhead. A tap made a juddering noise, as if there were not enough pressure.

'Julie! . . . Julie! . . . You've forgotten the napkins again, my girl . . .'

'Here they are, madame . . .'

Cool blasts, smelling of the drenched ground and cut hay, blew in through the door and the windows. It was still raining from time to time in large drops which formed a diagonal hatching, through which glinted occasional rays of sunshine.

'Do you mind sitting on the other side of the room? . . . This is the commander's table and it's time I laid it for dinner . . . Won't you finish your glass?'

Yes . . . No . . . He was more thirsty for a large glass of cold water and he dared not ask for one. What were they going to say to Mademoiselle? She would probably understand without there being any need to explain. She would put on a prim look. She would examine Marthe on the sly.

Cardinaud didn't know what to do with himself. His vitality was spent. He had come to the end, or rather almost to the end, of his task, and now this waiting left him as it were in the air. It was such an unpleasant sensation that he was relieved really to hear at last the sound of a car, an old car, and long before it stopped, outside the one-time mill, he was certain it was Gugusse's old crock.

They must have been making inquiries locally. As Dédé had said that morning, he knew the good spots where you can hear all that's going on.

They emerged from the car, both of them, and you could tell from Gugusse's stance that they had been drinking.

'Hey there, *patron* . . .'

Dédé was taking a look round the room and spotted Cardinaud.

'Here already, are you?'

His eyes grew hard. Gugusse, to whom he could not have told the whole truth, looked surprised.

'Who's he?'

Cardinaud had no weapon. He hadn't even got his coat on to give him some appearance of dignity and the colour from his braces had run onto his shirt, his trousers were clinging to his thighs, and when he walked, his shoes still squelched out muddy water.

He had no weapon of any sort. He had never fought. He had no wish to fight.

'. . . *girt in his only armour . . .*'

He had read those words somewhere. Was it in the Bible, in the New Testament? At all events it was connected with his Sundays at Notre-Dame de Bon Port . . . The text for one of the dean's sermons? . . .

Girt in his only armour . . .

'He's left . . .'

He waited there, standing up, defenceless, with his shirt stained and his hair stuck to his forehead.

'You told him, eh? . . .'

For the second time that day he swallowed hard and articulated uncertainly:

'Yes . . .'

One might have believed Dédé had the gift of second sight, since he asked the one question that could be of any importance.

'Has he got any money?'

'I gave him some . . .'

He could have made no reply, claimed that he didn't know. But he had to go through with it to the end, to the bitter end of his drama.

Dédé spat, looked at Gugusse in perplexity.

'How much?'

'About eight hundred . . .'

'I say, *patron*, when's there a train at Mareuil?'

The *patron* glanced up at the face of the clock.

'In half an hour, the local line to Sainte-Hermine . . .'

The family which was sheltering under the tree had come downstairs again, freshly spruced, and the children were already being sat down at the table.

'Julie! . . . Serve the soup for the little girl, will you? . . . Yesterday she . . .'

Dédé was paying for the drinks. He wore his most lowering expression. He was in no hurry to be gone. In the end, after walking right round the room, he came and planted himself in front of Cardinaud and puffed his drunken breath in his face.

'You, you can thank your lucky stars!'

Why lucky? That there were several people in the room? That the train is in only half an hour? That . . .

And before going to join Gugusse who was making his way back to the old car, Dédé added, after spitting once

118

more, in a low voice, but in a voice so full of contempt that Cardinaud would never forget it:

'You're a dirty little twerp . . .'

The '*mogettes*' couple came downstairs in their turn. The maid was speaking to Cardinaud.

'If you like to sit at this table . . . Red or white wine? . . . There's some Mareuil wine as well, ten sous extra . . .'

He dropped his head over his plate and his head was so heavy that he propped it up with both his hands.

'Aren't you having anything to eat?'

'I'm waiting for someone,' he said.

# CHAPTER EIGHT

HE heard footsteps on the gravel of the path, then the slight creaking of the hinges of the wicket-gate, and the next moment he saw her, he could observe her for a few seconds while she believed herself alone with her thoughts.

She was worried. Even as she closed the gate behind her, she seemed to be preparing the words she was shortly going to say and he would even have sworn that her lips were moving.

She was tired, rather pale, but she was very often like that. What struck him more was that her hair was in a mess, that little curls were straying down either side of her face, she who took such fanatical pains over the way her hair was done.

Her dress, which had been put to dry, was still rather creased, and like this, with her bag in her hand, her brows contracted, a sort of limpness in her bearing, she looked like a little housewife going to do her shopping.

He had to shift a foot. Though it made so slight a noise, she heard it, and she spoke entirely naturally as she looked around:

'That you?'

Then she caught sight of him between two bushes which the rain had lacquered to a dark green. She was taken by surprise, certainly; her face showed annoyance, but not as much as might have been expected. Perhaps she was telling herself that it was bound to happen some day or other. Might as well be straight away . . .

'Why have you come?'

Along the lane going down to the old mill, there were

couples every twenty yards or a family strolling gently along, so gently that at a distance the figures seemed to be motionless in the setting sun. And here they were, a couple amongst couples like any other. They, too, were strolling in the cool air after the storm, in the strong smell of the drenched earth, while drops of limpid water fell from one leaf onto another and the cracking of wood could be heard in the undergrowth.

Cardinaud had not the patience to wait for another question in order to say what he had to say and he spoke, gazing down on the ground to his left:

'He's gone . . .'

Was she expecting that too? Was it a relief for her? Her face still showed no expression, except of tiredness. She glanced at the bag she was holding in her hand. She said, listlessly:

'He hadn't any money . . .'

'I gave him some . . .'

This time she did look at him and it was he who turned his head away, because he could see she was humiliated. They were still walking, one pace at a time. The commander was going to come past them. She inquired in a low voice:

'Did he ask you for it?'

He nodded. He was cheating slightly. The facts were more complicated. But was it worth telling the whole story? Didn't this come to the same thing?

She was not crying. She was showing no reaction. What was going to become of her?

And he, so as to reassure her straight away, so as not to leave her in the air any longer:

'It's too late to go back home to-night . . .'

She looked at him again, rather taken aback.

'You think we'll have to . . .'

The commander, coming level with them, was gazing at them with an intentionally offensive stare. He must have been imagining things . . . He could be heard stopping later on to turn round.

'We had better find another hotel. Do you want to go and collect your suitcase?'

Once again, she whispered:

'You think so?'

She was looking at the vine-covered front of the building and made up her mind to go inside; her foot stumbled on the threshold, and he heard her saying:

'Julie, will you make out my bill . . .'

The birds were singing as if, after the storm, it were the start of a new day. Cardinaud caught himself lighting a cigarette. Marthe joined him again, carrying her suitcase, and he took it from her.

'Listen, Hubert, I'm wondering . . .'

He shook his head. She must not speak. It was pointless.

'You'll have to know . . .'

'I know . . . Don't let's talk about it any more . . .'

They looked just like any pair of people going to catch a train, except that there wasn't another train. In the streets of Mareuil, where the evening was beginning to shade out-lines over, people were out in the fresh air and almost all the women had slipped their hands, in a familiar move-ment, through the arms of their companions.

Marthe slipped her hand through, too, because she was weary.

'Where shall we go?'

'We'll go and see if they've still got a room at the "Green Oak" . . .'

He had said 'a room', hesitating slightly. He wanted to see if she would react, but she appeared not to notice it. Gugusse's car was no longer there. Four men were playing cards in the twilight and the hotel-keeper who was amongst them rose to his feet, and looked at the couple closely.

'If I'm not mistaken, it's Monsieur Cardinaud . . . How are you, seeing it's two years since we last met? . . . And

Madame Cardinaud! . . . You haven't brought the children? . . . You're probably only passing through?'

'Passing through, yes . . . Have you a room?'

'I've just got one left . . . And what's more, you've been lucky, since it was booked and if the guests hadn't . . .'

He asked Marthe:

'Wouldn't you like something to eat?'

'I've had dinner at my uncle's . . .'

True enough! There was that other question which would certainly have to be tackled one day, if only so as not to make a blunder when he next met the Tessons. What had she told them?

They climbed the stairs they had climbed before, when on holiday.

'I've nothing left looking onto the street, but you'll be all the quieter for it . . .'

It was soothing to be welcomed by this commonplace room, to open the shutters, to look out into the garden. Marthe did not dare get undressed. She didn't know what to do. She stood there, erect, as if paying a visit, and she could find nothing to say but:

'You're soaking . . . You'll catch a cold . . .'

He took off his coat.

'Hubert . . .'

But no! Nothing must be said but commonplace, nothing done but everyday actions, so as to grow used to each other again quite quietly.

'I've forgotten to ask what time we can catch a bus . . .'

He went downstairs. When he came up again, a few long minutes later, she was standing in front of the window, still in her hat, but she had placed her handbag on the table. She was looking outside. It was she who spoke, asking:

'What time?'

'The first one's at half-past eight . . .'

'Did you tell them to call us?'

'At seven o'clock . . .'

123

'Do you remember, Hubert? . . . When you talked about getting married to me, I said to you . . .'

She had said to him very precisely:

'*Do you believe you won't regret it one day?*'

She had added, thoughtfully:

'*I wonder if I wouldn't do better to . . .*'

To admit everything, no doubt? To tell him about Emile? To admit to him that . . .

He had stopped her talking. And later on, when they were married, he had suddenly felt sad at the very moment when he should have been his happiest, because his suspicion had become a certainty.

Marthe had been observing him . . . She had been wondering whether he would notice that he was not the first and he had said nothing, he had pretended to . . .

'Let's go to bed . . . It's late . . .'

To help her, he closed the shutters and refrained from switching on the lamp, with the result that they had no light but the mauve strip between the slats.

He lay right over to one side of the bed. He made no attempt to kiss her. He only murmured:

'Good night, Marthe . . .'

And she, wide awake:

'Good night . . . '

She had her eyes open, he could tell. She would not go to sleep for a long time, perhaps not all the night? But she was not crying. She was thinking.

She had been right when she had claimed, once, that he didn't really know her. He had lived beside her, he had given her two children, he talked to her, he kissed her, they made plans together, and he never knew that one day it would need only Emile's return, filthy, shrunken, surly, wretched, for her to follow him as a bitch follows her master.

It was not her fault.

'Are you asleep?' he asked very softly.

She made no reply, but he knew she was not asleep. The proof was that, a little later, he felt her hand near his, and then two fingers timidly squeezing his finger.

The storm on Thursday had confounded the weather, for the rest of the season some maintained, and the sky was lowering, a luminous grey which hurt the eyes more than full sunlight.

Cardinaud was standing in his pew, more erect, more stiffly than usual, and he was staring intently at the yellow flames of the candles; he was conscientiously blending his voice with the voices of the choristers and the organ, and from time to time he bent down to make his son keep still.

'*Agnus Dei, qui tollis peccata mundi . . .*'

He knew that if some people were turning round, it was to look at him. That was why he was holding himself so erect. That was why he had to be even more his usual self than ever.

On the way out he was exchanging greetings . . .

'Good morning Monsieur Cardinaud . . .'

'Good morning, madame . . . Good morning, monsieur . . .'

What did it matter that they were whispering:

'It's young Cardinaud . . . His wife's come back . . . Apparently . . .'

'Pick up your feet as you walk, Jean . . .'

He met his sister-in-law, Juliette, doing her shopping.

'Good morning, Hubert . . . How are you? . . . And . . .'

A tiny hesitation. Why?

'And your wife?'

'She's very well, thanks . . .'

'Have you kept the governess?'

'No . . .'

He had called at his home, in the Rue de la Pie. He had sat down for a while in the cellar-kitchen. He had to. It was difficult, the first few days. But afterwards . . .

Marthe must purposely have placed the contents of her handbag on the mantelpiece, in the bedroom: her identity papers and more than five thousand francs. When she had seen him looking, she had murmured:

'I'll have to send them back to my uncle in a few days' time . . . I told him . . .'

He trembled. He felt afraid.

'. . . that we needed it for an operation . . .'

There! It was finished, now! The worst was over! She had been to her uncle's, and while Emile was waiting in the old mill, she had told him this story . . .

Perhaps she had added that it was one of the children who was ill?

It was finished! Finished!

That same morning, before leaving to go to Mass, Cardinaud had taken the last step that remained to be taken. He had left in full view the newspaper that carried the story:

'A railway employee yesterday discovered the corpse of an unknown man who had suffered numerous stab wounds, in a ditch behind the station at La Roche-sur-Yon. The following description is given of the victim who appears to be a stranger to the district and had no identity papers: height . . .'

'Hi! Cardinaud . . .'

A car gliding noiselessly along had stopped near by. Monsieur Mandine was hailing him, sticking an arm out of the window.

'He's a big fellow, your boy! . . . I say, I can rely on you to-morrow, can't I? . . .'

'Of course, Monsieur Mandine . . .'

'By the bye . . . Is it true, what I've been told . . .?'

'My wife's come home, yes . . .'

The other man was looking at him with surprise, with a

hint of respect and of commiseration combined. What should he have said? Should he have congratulated him? He was starting his engine again and calling out bluffly:

'Ah, well! It's all to the good . . . I'm glad for your sake . . . See you to-morrow, Cardinaud . . . We'll have to have a chat about that Duvallet business; it's not working out quite right . . . Enjoy your Sunday . . . !'

There! He had worked out what he had had to do, all by himself. He was going along the Remblai, as on every Sunday. The sea was grey, the sky grey. Was it perhaps going to rain towards the end of the day?

'Same as usual, Monsieur Cardinaud?'

'A vermouth, yes . . . And a redcurrant syrup for the youngster . . .'

'Please, Daddy . . . Where's Mademoiselle gone?'

'I don't know . . .'

'Who does know?'

'Nobody . . .'

The orchestra was playing *The Merry Widow*. He would next have to go and fetch the Sunday cake from the Mesdemoiselles Dufours, hold it straight, by the red string . . .

Nothing would be changed, nothing had changed. He still walked with the same step, raised his hat in the same style.

'What are you doing, Dad?'

Nothing . . . He had just forgotten, quite simply, forgotten to go on living . . . He had stopped, there, on the pavement, like a machine . . .

'Come on . . .'

It would not happen to him again. He would take care of that.

'What are we going to have for lunch?'

'Roast meat and fried potatoes . . .'

'Who's doing the fried potatoes?'

'Mummy is . . .'

'Where shall we go for our walk to-day?'

'To La Rudelière . . .'

He greeted Mademoiselle Julienne as she came out of her house, and she returned his greeting rather curtly. Then he felt for his key in his pocket, and bent down ever so slightly to look the whole length of the passage through the keyhole.

The oil in the frying-pan was spitting. Marthe was basting the joint with boiling hot butter.

'Don't come in the kitchen in your nice suit, Jean . . . Ask your father to put your old smock on for you . . .'

There.

The newspaper was no longer in its place.

It was finished. It was enough just to go carefully, like convalescents taking their first few steps.

'You didn't forget the cake . . . That's good . . .'

He took off his jacket and went out, in his shirt-sleeves, to smoke a cigarette in the yard.

*Fontenay-le-Comte, 22 July, 1941.*